BRAZEN

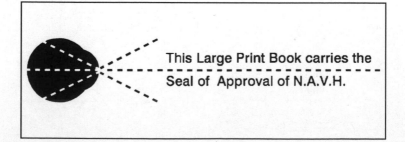

This Large Print Book carries the
Seal of Approval of N.A.V.H.

A VALENTINO MYSTERY

BRAZEN

LOREN D. ESTLEMAN

THORNDIKE PRESS
A part of Gale, Cengage Learning

GALE
CENGAGE Learning·

Farmington Hills, Mich • San Francisco • New York • Waterville, Maine
Meriden, Conn • Mason, Ohio • Chicago

GALE
CENGAGE Learning·

LIBRARY OF CONGRESS CATALOGING-IN-PUBLICATION DATA

Names: Estleman, Loren D., author.
Title: Brazen : a Valentino mystery / by Loren D. Estleman.
Description: Waterville, Maine : Thorndike Press, 2017. | Series: Thorndike Press large print mystery
Identifiers: LCCN 2016048532| ISBN 9781410495235 (hardcover) | ISBN 141049523X (hardcover)
Subjects: LCSH: Large type books. | GSAFD: Mystery fiction.
Classification: LCC PS3555.S84 B737 2017 | DDC 813/.54—dc23
LC record available at https://lccn.loc.gov/2016048532

Published in 2017 by arrangement with Tom Doherty Associates

Printed in Mexico
1 2 3 4 5 6 7 21 20 19 18 17

In memoriam
Debbie Bratcher
When I feel the need to be good,
she's my model.

It was a blonde. A blonde to make a bishop kick a hole in a stained glass window.

— Raymond Chandler,
Farewell, My Lovely (1940)

You know, it isn't that gentlemen really prefer blondes. It's just that we look dumber.

— Ginger Rogers,
Follow the Fleet (1936)

■ ■ ■ ■

I
GENTLEMEN PREFER
BLONDES

■ ■ ■ ■

1

Kyle Broadhead looped a giant rubber band on the toe of his wingtip, aimed his leg at a picture of the director of the UCLA board of regents shaking his hand, drew the band taut, and let go. It zinged through the air of his office and struck the protective glass a tremendous whack, but failed to crack it.

"Plexiglas." He snorted. "I might have guessed. The cheap so-and-so."

"Why hang it at all, if you dislike him so much?" Valentino asked.

"I need the target practice."

"One of these days you're going to snort yourself into a case of sudden retirement."

"Never. I am an ornament of this institution."

"Make yourself more useful than one. You know how to tie one of these things."

The professor looked up at his visitor, in a dinner jacket with both ends of his bow tie hanging loose.

"How come Dean Martin died again and no one told me?"

"It's a party. Even here they throw them sometimes without writing 'Torn jeans optional' on the invitation. Seriously, if you don't help me out I'm going for a clip-on."

"Why stop there? Get one of those elastic things, so you can stretch it out and let it snap back when you tell a joke. Better yet, get one with a motor that makes it spin. Come to think of it, I'll pick one up for myself. I can distract the next moneybags host while I spit those godawful cheese puffs into my napkin, then make my pitch for a donation."

"Kyle!"

"Keep your shirtboard on." The old academic got up from his desk, stepped behind the young film archivist, circled his arms around his neck, and tied. "What's the occasion, and why wasn't I invited?"

"Dinner party at Beata Limerick's, to celebrate her newest acquisition. A cozy little affair of sixty or so. That's as many as can stand on her balcony without finishing up in the middle of Wilshire Boulevard. As for why you aren't on the list, you'll have to take that up with Beata."

"No need. You just told me."

"Told you what? You get along fine with her."

"Her, yes. Heights, no. If God had meant people to live in penthouses, He would have given them parachutes."

"That's the first time I've ever heard you admit you were afraid of anything."

"I confess to frailty on a case-by-case basis. Let's keep this one between you, me, and the Lady Limerick. If Mr. Plexiglas gets wind of it, he'll hold the next meeting in the Watts Tower."

"Why'd you tell Beata?"

"I had to come clean the third time she asked me over. Contrary to the prevailing theory, I'm only rude to my close friends. There." He spread his hands and circled in front of Valentino to inspect the result. "If you ever hope to replace me as this university's chief procurer, you're going to have to stop renting your tuxes out of Shifty Louie's trunk in the parking lot. All you need in that getup is a towel on your arm and a phony French accent."

"I'd make a better maitre d' than a fundraiser. I can twist a corkscrew, but not somebody's arm. And I can't make a bow out of a wet noodle."

"Who said anything about a maitre d'? You always did aim too high."

13

"Well, I'm off."

"This time I hope you at least come back wearing a chinchilla coat."

"Vicuna," Valentino said. "It was a vicuna coat Gloria Swanson gave William Holden in *Sunset Boulevard.* And our relationship isn't like that."

"I don't know why not. She signs one check, and that wet dream of an architectural project of yours rises fully intact from a cloud of dust, like in a cartoon."

"I wouldn't ask, and she wouldn't offer, with or without the sordid details. She knows what it means to haul yourself up by your own bootstraps."

"She should know. She married the guy who bought her the boots."

It was true, to an extent. Beata Limerick had turned her back on stardom and fallen into a fortune.

That, at least, was the line taken by every feature writer in L.A. who'd succeeded in storming her parapets and scoring an interview, and from Valentino's personal experience, he found no reason to question it. A town that chewed up and spat out female talent the moment it turned forty had no mercy for those who beat it to the punch, but she had done more than that; she'd rubbed its face in it and made it like it.

Metro-Goldwyn-Mayer had been giving her the big buildup in 1967 ("Not since Marilyn . . .") when she walked out on her contract, offering no explanation. The studio sued, then withdrew its suit when she handed the head of production a cashier's check for the entire amount she'd been paid while on salary. The money was accepted, but not before a toady for Louis B. Mayer actually spoke the words, "You'll never work in this town again."

She never did; but then she never had to.

Six months after she quit, she married the chairman of the board of the corporation that built Century City. When he died, shortly before their fifth anniversary, he left her forty million dollars in cash and securities, a controlling interest in the corporation, and an additional sixteen million in real property, including four hundred feet fronting on Rodeo Drive in Beverly Hills. She entered probate a grieving widow and emerged a charter member of an exclusive club: Together with Mae West and Greta Garbo, the former Bertha Liechtenstein of Santa Rosa (population 10,773), owned the largest tract of Southern California in private hands.

"I've even got a name for it," she declared,

15

with a chortle: "The Richest Bitches in Britches."

They were standing on the balcony of her penthouse in Beverly Hills, looking out at the dusting of lights that was Los Angeles on a night swept clean of yellow-ocher auto exhaust. On evenings like that the horizon vanished, the hundreds of thousands of electric bulbs merging with the stars so that the city seemed folded in the firmament. She wore a low-cut evening gown and a wrap filmy enough to create the illusion of transparency, but opaque enough to filter out the effects of seventy-plus years on bare shoulders and bosom. Through it glittered the facets of a diamond choker, her only jewelry tonight, apart from the wedding set that had resided on her left hand for five decades.

Valentino had lied to Broadhead about the number of guests, knowing his mentor would never have let up on the gigolo jokes had he known there was only one.

"I don't believe you," he told her. "Kyle says only sane people question their own sanity, and no woman who is truly a bitch would admit to it."

She smiled. It was an attractive smile, if a bit sad, and her bones were good. Time, not surgery, had been kind to the woman whom

Hedda Hopper had declared "Hollywood's Alice Roosevelt Longworth." She was a force to reckon with at elegant parties. Coat-check girls who wanted to be starlets, starlets who wanted to be stars, and stars who didn't want to be coat-check girls laughed at her jokes and gushed over her taste in clothing and jewelry, and came away uncertain whether they should worry more about Beata's discussing them behind their backs or not discussing them at all.

"Dear boy. You'll never be a grown-up until you stop warming over the wisdom of others. I had my coming of age at sixty, when I realized that half of what I knew I'd been told by Pietro."

Pietro Jacobelli, squat voluptuary that he was, had been the Prince Charming who'd rescued her from cautionary-tale hell. Their marriage had been looked upon at first as the usual merger of beauty and loot, but brief as it was, it had proven to be the genuine article. She'd never remarried, although she'd been proposed to by men who could have increased her fortune many times over.

"He was just sixty when he left me," she said. "Everything since then I went out and learned myself."

"I have time, then," Valentino said.

"Not as much as you think; which is the reason I wonder why you're wasting it." She laid her hand atop his where it rested on the balcony's marble railing. "Why don't you let me build that theater for you?"

2

"Beata, we've been through this. You know what people will say."

"I'm too old to care about that," she said. "*I'm* not."

Specifically, he was thinking of what Kyle Broadhead would say. The old curmudgeon was only kidding when he made remarks about Valentino's relationship with the former actress, but he would suspect there was a great deal more to it if his colleague came away from the evening with the wherewithal to finish restoring The Oracle, the classic motion-picture palace Valentino called home.

Both he and Beata knew that there was nothing seamy about her offer. All she cared for was companionship; but try selling that one to the professor, or for that matter anyone else in that jaded town.

She liked him, he knew, because he was the only one in her circle who didn't care

19

what she said about him or if she said nothing. He had no social aspirations beyond his relationship with Harriet Johansen, the woman to whom he was faithful, and no ambitions beyond finishing The Oracle — a time-consuming and hideously expensive hobby — and rescuing classic films from obscurity, which helped to finance it. She had tested him, found he wanted nothing from her but the pleasure of her company, and met with him often to compare their latest treasures, celebrate their victories, and commiserate over their defeats. They shared a keen interest in Hollywood's rich and gaudy history. For his part, it was his job: He was an archivist with UCLA's Department of Film Preservation. For hers, it was a passion: She was the foremost collector of movie memorabilia on the West Coast.

With one bid at Sotheby's — a cool million for the drapery-dress Vivien Leigh had worn in *Gone with the Wind* — Beata Limerick had raised the bar on everything from Mickey Rooney's Andy Hardy hat to the chariot Charlton Heston had raced in *Ben-Hur.* It had made her no friends in the collecting community, but it removed any onus of competition between her and Valentino, as every penny he earned went into the theater renovation, and he'd sold off his own modest collection in order to keep it going. His acquisitive interest now was confined to film itself, on behalf of the university that supported him.

They were serious rivals once only, before they became friends. She'd annihilated him in a battle over an unedited print of *The Sandpiper* at Elizabeth Taylor's estate auction. That was the first day they'd lunched; her treat.

"I couldn't resist," she'd said. "I doubled Liz Taylor in that one — it was my brunette period — and it's all I have to show for my career in pictures, such as it was. Anyway, you're better off without it. It's a stinker."

"Stinkers have a way of making money. Burton and Taylor are a kitschy gold mine. We could have exhibited it in revival houses and made enough to restore half a dozen better films."

"I'll make it up to you one day."

At the time, he'd thought it an empty promise. He'd yet to make his mark in his chosen trade. Now, with some significant notches on his belt, he wondered if that day had come. Certainly she didn't want to let go of the possibility.

"At least let me contribute to your cause," she said. "During the bad old days of the blacklist, I helped a number of set designers establish themselves in the contracting trade. One or two of them are still active. I can arrange for you to obtain some material at cost; less, perhaps."

He sipped pink champagne, her libation of choice. "It's tempting; but the result would be the same. They'll wonder why you waited so long to cash in, and why you selected me as the benefactor."

"Well, then, we might as well sleep together and get it over with."

He sprayed champagne.

Her cook, a Jamaican named Mrs. Flynn, with whom her mistress had been squabbling for forty years, had laid out a feast before going home: squabs stuffed with wild rice and shallots, new potatoes, kale served with raspberry dressing, and crème brûlée for dessert. Beata insisted that squab was to be eaten without utensils. Her fingers dissected her bird with fastidious efficiency.

"MGM drilled me as if for a coronation," she said. "They had Russian counts on staff. It went beyond singing and dancing lessons. They taught us to dress, speak, which fork to use, when to dispense with one entirely, and how to take charge of interviews. Last week I heard a male star on *The View* compare the size of his organ to a snow pea.

That couldn't happen in the old days. The studio was a duchy, with its own government, army, and fire department. My dear, it was the Vatican! When Robert Taylor went to Universal, he didn't know how to pick up a phone and make a dinner reservation. There had always been someone to take care of such things at Tiffany's." Which was her private, semi-affectionate euphemism for Metro-Goldwyn-Mayer.

"Is that why you dropped out?"

She ate, blue eyes twinkling in their thicket of creases. "I've been wondering when you'd get around to that: The Secret of Beata Limerick."

"I'm sorry. I shouldn't pry into your personal affairs."

"Bullshit. What else do friends have to talk about? I hate to disappoint you, but there's no mystery about it. It's just easier to refuse to answer the question than it is to repeat the same story over and over. What's dismissed as egocentricity in youth, therefore pardonable, is a bore in old age, and intolerable. I was afraid of the curse."

"What curse?" He put down his fork. His fingers lacked the dexterity of her long slender digits.

"The *curse,* foolish boy. Thelma Todd. Jean Harlow. Marilyn, who might as well

23

claim ownership. It was still around for Sharon Tate. All the great blond bombshells came to an early end. I was twenty-five; if I wasn't going to be one of the great brazen hussies of Hollywood, the hell with it, and I didn't want to die. When that truck took off Jayne Mansfield's head, I got the message loud and clear. I didn't walk away from my destiny, as the tabloids are so fond of repeating. I ran for my life."

"She wasn't really decapitated, you know. It was just her wig they found on the hood of her Buick."

She reached across the table to pat his hand. There wasn't a scrap of grease on hers.

"I was being grotesque for a point. Is she any less dead?"

"You seriously believe there's a curse on blondes in the industry?"

"Not all of them, only the ones who rose to the level of an icon. Teri Garr and Melanie Griffith haven't a thing to worry about. And I'm not the only one who skedaddled. I've talked with Mamie about it."

Now that he thought of it, Mamie Van Doren had quit about the same time. "I'd heard she was something of a ditz on the occult. I thought you were more level-headed."

"Just because I don't proselytize doesn't mean I'm not a believer. I'm into astrology, tarot cards, and voodoo. It's my birthright. I'm a native Californian."

He sought to change a subject he found embarrassing. He didn't have to search for long. Most of the apartment was one huge room, partitions having been removed to create space for some of the artifacts she'd amassed. Opposite the heavily reinforced shelves and original posters in archival frames, a blue cloth covered something squarish on a sleek table with curving glass legs.

She followed the course of his gaze. "You're right, it's what I invited you here to see. Trust a detective like you to spot it."

"I'm all aquiver."

She rose gracefully, with none of the hitches connected with gravity and imperfect circulation, and led the way across a carpet as thick as a mattress. With a trilly little, "Ta-da!" — her vocal training was still paying off — she snatched away the cloth.

A square glass case displayed a mass of what looked like pink cotton candy on a mannequin head.

"Is that — ?" A sudden chill prevented him from finishing the sentence.

"The same. It's why what you said before

was no news to me, and why I steered the conversation in the direction I did. You can take the queen out of the drama but not the drama out of the queen."

Beyond doubt, the object in the case was Jayne Mansfield's infamous wig, the very one that had been recovered from the hood of her smashed Buick.

"I got it at Christie's," she said. "The last owner bought it in a lot when the New Orleans Police Department cleared out its evidence room after Hurricane Katrina. I'd've gotten the Buick, too, if that sprout Spielberg hadn't outbid me."

3

A decidedly less exotic brand of champagne was available a few days later. It was bottled in Schenectady, New York, and poured into plastic flutes that came in two pieces and had to be assembled by the host.

"Hump!" Broadhead adjusted his readers to peer at the bottle. "It says here if you send in ten labels, the manufacturer will respond with an autographed photo of the founder of the distillery, a *Monsieur* Harvey Finkbeiner."

Valentino said, "It doesn't say that at all!"

"It should include a coupon for a free stomach pump."

"It was a contest between Dom Pérignon and sixteen cases of LED lights. Technology won."

They were standing on the sidewalk in front of The Oracle: the owner; his girl-friend, Harriet; his disgruntled mentor; Fanta, soon-to-be Mrs. Disgruntled Mentor; Smith Oldfield; and Henry Anklemire. Oldfield, the ivy-covered legal advisor to the Film Preservation Department, and Anklemire, the flack in charge of Information Services, had earned the privilege of attendance through Oldfield's proofing of the tons of documents required to take possession of the property and to arrange the cooperation of the various contractors, and Anklemire's tireless efforts to promote public interest in the films Valentino managed to free from Purgatory.

The only no-show was Leo Kalishnikov, the brilliant, eccentric theater designer who had overseen the project from the start. He was in Prague, collaborating with an expatriate film director currently under indictment for U.S. tax evasion on a media center the director wanted to install in the basement of the sixteenth-century church he was converting into a private house. But the absent guest had commemorated the occasion with a congratulatory text:

TRY NOT TO ELECTROCUTE YOUR-SELF. LOVE, L. K.

"What are we waiting for? It's dark enough." Harriet, in a sleeveless blouse and chambray bell-bottoms, hugged herself. It was an uncharacteristically chilly night in West Hollywood.

Valentino shrugged out of his windbreaker and draped it over her bare shoulders. "The electrician. The insurance company threatened to void the policy if I throw the switch without him present. Also he's got the remote."

Above them, vanishing into gathering dusk, towered The Oracle's marquee, dark for decades.

"If this is going to be a replay of *Christmas Vacation,* I vote we open the champagne now."

"Kyle, be nice." Fanta used the singsong tone she brought out when her fiancé needed upbraiding.

Anklemire adjusted his hairpiece, a discard from Kevin Spacey's last feature. He was a short man in a suit that needed no outside illumination. "I still think we should've invited the press. I got a producer with *Access Hollywood* laid in Salt Lake City. That's like finding a chocolate Easter bunny in Tehran."

"Let's save that gem for when we really need it." Oldfield, it was said, spent time each month collecting the names of possible character witnesses to speak up for Anklemire at his inevitable procurement trial.

Fanta, herself an attorney in training, asked Valentino if he was sure the wiring was safe. "With Mr. Oldfield and me here, I'm not sure about the ethics of either of us defending you from a personal-injury suit."

Broadhead said, "I think I resent that."

"I didn't mean you," she said. "If you took Val to court, you'd never see me naked again. I'm talking about the odd innocent passerby."

"I'll grant you the 'odd,' " he said. "I'll get back to you on the 'innocent.' I've lived in the City of Angels long enough to shoot craps with Gabriel."

Anklemire frowned. "That ain't nice, Professor. And I'm Jewish."

"Mea culpa."

"No, thanks. I et already."

"Where's that electrician?" Harriet demanded. "We're about to go into *Who's on First.*"

Just then the man himself arrived, a smiling black man wearing gray coveralls and carrying a steel toolbox with a rubber-covered handle. He shook Valentino's hand and looked up at the marquee.

"It was a bitch," he said. "My crew had to sit on their fannies for a month waiting for the go-ahead from the EPA on asbestos removal, and *then* six weeks haggling with

30

OSHA and the insurance company. And the wires? I had to go to my old man in the nursing home to ask him about the wires. He said that gauge went out with Tom Edison. We had to rip them all out, even the ones that were good as new, because they wouldn't splice with the replacements. But you'll be glad I talked you into those LEDs. They'll pay for themselves in a year. You can leave them on all night for pennies."

Valentino turned out his jeans pockets. "You're welcome to all those I've got left."

"Val," Harriet said, "I'm weighing a brain in an hour. And I can't feel my feet." She was a Crime Scene Investigator with the Los Angeles Police Department.

He nodded, and looked at the electrician, who lowered his toolbox to the sidewalk, knelt, opened it, and handed him a slim black remote-control box from inside.

Valentino squared his shoulders, planted his feet wide, glanced toward Fanta focusing on the marquee with a camera phone, extended the remote at arm's length, hesitated a beat, and pressed the POWER button.

A bulb halfway up the structure glowed briefly and went out with a sigh.

The silence that followed was broken by someone's throat clearing.

"Breathtaking." Broadhead popped the cork on the bottle of champagne.

The party reconvened in the theater's unfinished lobby, the electrician remaining outside to consult his schematics sheet. Dust cloths covered the candy counter and old-fashioned popcorn cart. Faux marble tiles covered half the floor; the rest was plywood, and had been for weeks, awaiting more tiles. Somewhere in the world, Valentino was certain, people were tripping over tiles, boxes and boxes of tiles; cursing them, using them for bases in games of softball, skipping them like flat stones across the surfaces of lakes, while the floor in the lobby of The Oracle yawned and scratched itself, waiting for someone to come along and dress it, like some bored French king.

"It's probably just like Christmas-tree bulbs," Anklemire offered. "If one goes out —" He shrugged and slurped from his flute.

Harriet said, "Cheer up, Val. Two steps forward, one step back. Not so long ago it was the other way around."

"Let's talk about something else." He told them about the latest item in Beata Limerick's collection.

Harriet shrugged out of his windbreaker. "Good God. That would freak out my section chief, and he brings liverwurst sandwiches to the scenes of gang slayings."

Others responded according to their kind. Smith Oldfield:

"I wonder if Mariska Hargitay is aware of this. It would seem to me an item like that would rightfully belong to the daughter of the deceased."

Henry Anklemire:

"I'm seeing a picture of Hargitay with the wig in *Variety,* and a little mention that the current owner is friends with a member of the Film Preservation Department."

Kyle Broadhead:

"I don't see anything unusual about it. The closer one gets to death, the more fascinated he is by it."

Fanta said, "If you don't stop that kind of talk, I'm going to have my mother pull strings and invite the president to our wedding. You can deal with the Secret Service and bomb-sniffing dogs." The bride-to-be's mother was an ambassador.

He shuddered. "And I haven't voted since Abe Abolafia ran on the nudist ticket."

Harriet, leaning against the ticket booth, sipped champagne. "I'm with Fanta. Val, your associations are becoming morbid."

"This from a woman who weighs brains for a living," Broadhead said.

Valentino said, "I have to go back. She's promised to sell me her master print of *The Sandpiper* for what she paid for it five years ago."

"What's that?" Anklemire asked.

He told him.

The P.R. man rubbed his hands. "Taylor and Burton? I can smell the money!"

Broadhead told him he could smell money from outer space.

The electrician came in, carrying his toolbox. "If you folks are waiting for me, you might as well go home. I have to assemble my crew and inspect every inch of the wiring for breaks or frays. That'll take the rest of the week."

"Pour the man some champagne," Broadhead said. "I can hear it going flat in the bottle."

4

The invitation was for two o'clock Tuesday. Beata had promised him Mrs. Flynn's salmon mousse, with green beans in white wine sauce and sour-apple tarts. At the hour mentioned, Valentino came off the elevator and read the old lady's hasty hand on a page of personal stationery thumbtacked to the door:

V. —
Let yourself in and sit down on something. I'm putting on my face, and no man should be left to stand that long.

Love, B.

Classic Beata.

Placing the package he'd brought under one arm, he opened the door. The two flat cans bound in bright silver paper contained Beata's MGM screen test, which he'd acquired in a blind lot along with some more commercial items, and had been saving for a special occasion. Such items were a rare find; the studios routinely incinerated them when a career proved stillborn. The reels seemed a more appropriate hostess gift than an ordinary bottle of wine.

A fifty-year-old Bell & Howell projector in excellent condition stood on a stout table facing a portable screen. It was a feature new to the apartment. He envied her contacts; it had taken him two years to track one down for The Oracle, and he craved another so he could screen early 3-D, which he thought superior to its high-tech modern counterpart. He set his package on an eight-foot chaise Hedy Lamarr had reclined on in *Samson and Delilah* — Beata's tastes were a shepherd's pie of flabby biblical epics, fantasy, *noir,* and lavish trash — and examined the stenciling on one of the film cans stacked on the carpet at the foot of the table: *The Sandpiper,* together with its production number and a stern warning that it was the property of Metro-Goldwyn-Mayer and was not to be removed from the studio.

Not a caveat to be taken lightly. Eddie Mannix, the head of security in those days, was still a suspect in the mysterious death of George Reeves, TV's first Superman.

Despite his disparagement of its worth to the history of cinema, the find excited Valentino. In his world, anything on celluloid was worth preserving (porno and the Dagwood-and-Blondie series excepted), and the prospect of obtaining a Metrocolor print in like-new condition intoxicated him.

"They're prone to bleeding," he'd told his friend, when she'd offered the film to him.

"So are old actresses. We'll screen it over the salmon and you can judge it for yourself."

She belonged to a generation of actors that rose late when they were between pictures, breakfasted in bed at eleven, lunched at midafternoon, and supped at eight before caravanning to the Mocambo, to lay the day to rest at dawn. He was accustomed to dining earlier. The delicate aroma of the entrée coming from the kitchen made his stomach rumble. The cook, he knew, would have left; she disliked being complimented, considering a dish prepared properly its own reward. Just as pleasantly, music was floating from the door of the bedroom.

Identifying the melody helped distract him from his hunger. It was "Diamonds Are a Girl's Best Friend," Marilyn Monroe's show-stopping production number from

Gentlemen Prefer Blondes; the old vixen's sense of humor at its most typical. Her comments on the Curse of Marilyn were still fresh in his mind. He still wasn't sure she'd bought into that old chestnut. In a city built of irony, he pictured himself its sole literal-minded resident.

Of all the storied bric-a-brac in her collection, he found two items most amusing: Margaret Hamilton's pointed witch's hat from *The Wizard of Oz* and Fred MacMurray's crutches from *Double Indemnity,* identified with hand-lettered 3×5 index cards along with the date she'd acquired them, and letters of provenance whose signatures alone were collectable: Judy Garland and Billy Wilder. Only someone of her temperament would juxtapose those two films. She was equal parts gaudy flash and disturbing dark matter; yet, oddly, not bipolar. She never dwelt in either world long enough to obsess over it.

He returned Francis Lederer's ruby ring from *The Return of Dracula* to its plush-lined box and looked at his watch: 2:21. Beata was rarely more than five minutes late for an appointment. She'd have no one accusing her of behaving like a diva; and she'd consider it a sin to allow one of Mrs. Flynn's masterpieces to grow cold and have to be

38

reheated.

The smell from the kitchen turned acrid.

A loud, razzing noise drowned out Marilyn, who seemed to be singing on a continuous loop, returning to the beginning of "Diamonds" immediately after the closing bars.

It was a smoke alarm.

Beata would never have left a meal meant for a guest unattended in the oven.

Valentino pushed through the swinging door. The kitchen was filled with smoke.

Coughing, eyes stinging, he stumbled across to the stove, flung open the oven door, releasing yet more smoke, groped for a pot holder, and swung the smoldering pan from the rack to the top of the range. He turned off the oven and switched on the fan in the overhead ventilator.

The smoke began to thin out. He snatched up a dish towel and snapped it, bullfighter fashion, at the saucer-shaped alarm mounted on the ceiling. After a minute the noise stopped.

". . . I don't mean rhinestones! Diamonds . . ."

He passed through the living room, following the sound of Marilyn Monroe's kittenlike voice, and rapped on the bedroom door; pounded on it with his fist. There was

39

nothing wrong with Beata's hearing, he knew. She had to have heard the alarm even if she'd failed to smell the smoke.

No response. He tried the knob. The door was locked. He banged again, hard enough to make it bounce in its frame, and called her name. He got nothing but silence from the other side.

Well, the worst that could happen was he'd catch her completely clothed except for one eyelash and she'd accuse him of watching too many John Wayne movies.

He'd never broken down a door. It always looked easy on-screen, but he knew that in real life they were never built of breakaway balsa. He backed off two steps and threw all his weight against the panels. His shoulder gave; they didn't. He switched to the one that wasn't throbbing and tried again. Two more attempts and one giant bruise later, the frame split and the door flew open. He almost fell under his own momentum, but caught himself in time to keep from sprawling across Beata's king-size bed, which already contained Beata herself.

She lay on her stomach, diagonally across the pearl-colored satin comforter, clutching the receiver of a white French-type telephone (perversely, visions of *Ninotchka* and

An American in Paris fluttered through his head) at the end of one outstretched arm. Her hair, which she'd continued to tint a soft yellow against relentless graying, was disheveled as in sleep, obscuring her profile. There were age spots on her shoulders and her skin sagged in places, but she was in remarkably good condition for a woman even much younger ("Pilates, dear boy; and the number on speed-dial of the best lift man in the Beverly Hills medical directory"). A CD player built into the wall facing the bed continued to belt out Norma Jean Baker's anthem for gold diggers from speakers concealed in twin framed monochrome photos of the Eiffel Tower; but Beata Limerick wasn't listening.

She was dead, which was shocking enough. Even more shocking, she was stark naked.

5

"What is it with you?" asked the man from Homicide.

Valentino hesitated. "I don't know how to answer that question."

"Cops talk to each other, you know. Sergeant Clifford with the LAPD told me that picture house you bought on West Hollywood came with a skeleton."

"The person who belonged to it was dead before I was born."

"The boys in San Diego said you were the last one to talk to a washed-up actor before he was beaten to death by Mike Grundage's gorillas."

"I think that honor goes to the gorillas."

"Last year, a cowboy star blew his brains out over a film you dug up for him."

"That was his decision. And I didn't dig up the film. Someone else did."

"You were first on the scene when a bil-lionaire movie collector shot his secretary to death. I was the lucky investigator in that one."

"You arrested the killer. It wasn't me."

"That's why I asked what is it with you. When the squeal came in on a has-been movie queen found dead in her bed, I don't know why I didn't think of you right off. You go through Hollywood like a snootful of coke."

"I wish I knew the answer, Lieutenant."

"If I was Marshal Dillon I'd run you out of the county. The murder rate would drop ten percent, among the movie crowd any-how."

"That's not fair."

"What would be, five? What we got?" Lieutenant Ray Padilla stuck his limp unlit cigarette back between his lips as if to keep air from leaking out.

A young officer in a trim uniform read aloud from a spiral pad.

The plainclothesman — and the clothes were indeed plain, to the point of nonexistence — circled the bed while the report droned on, studying the corpse with neutral-colored eyes and committing every detail to memory. Valentino knew him. Ray Padilla had passed out of his polyester period, but his gray suit, white shirt, and perfunctorily knotted blue necktie seemed as disconnected from the rumpled creature inside as a space suit; one imagined him climbing into it and buckling it up the back. That he managed, despite his clear disdain for appearances, to hold high rank in posh Beverly Hills said a great deal about his value to the department.

"Shut that damn thing off," he said when the officer finished reading.

That party glanced uncertainly at the CD, which was still playing the same song. "Lab rats don't like us touching anything, L. T."

"Use your elbow, and quick. I'd rather listen to a loose fan belt."

Marilyn stopped singing. The sudden silence was like a sharp cuff to the ears. The song had been playing so long Valentino had ceased to hear it.

Padilla completed his circuit. In true movie star fashion, the bed was situated in the center of the room. Beata's lifeless, naked body had begun to take on the quality of one of the figures in the Hollywood Wax Museum; or so Valentino fancied. Less than an hour had passed since he'd called 911 from the extension in the living room. He'd resisted the urge to cover his friend with the pale bedspread, knowing it would annoy the police and arouse their suspicion, if not actually invite a threat of charging him with tampering with a crime scene. But it bothered him, and after making the call he hadn't returned to the room until the police came.

Was it a crime scene? He'd seen no signs of violence and had felt no desire to investigate beyond what he'd seen at first glance. The woman was in her seventies, after all. There was no reason to believe she hadn't expired of natural causes. She had no enemies, not counting those collectors she'd beaten to the bottom line at auction (souls too timid to trash-talk her except behind her back), and nothing appeared to be missing from the apartment, even that grotesque artifact Jayne Mansfield had been wearing when she was killed. The only sign of turmoil was the ruined dish in the kitchen. It was merely routine that the local Homicide squad would be called upon to eliminate the possibility of foul play.

And yet there was something eerily familiar about the tableau that nudged at the edge of the film archivist's subconscious. He was still in too much shock to identify it, but the answer was as naggingly close as it was infuriatingly elusive.

The lieutenant stopped to bend close to the telephone receiver clenched in the dead woman's hand. The instrument was an original, not a replica — the rotary dial was a dead giveaway — whose cord plugged into a jack in the floor. Having decided where the bed would be placed, she'd have arranged the unconventional installation to avoid tripping over a cord attached to the wall.

Padilla cocked his ear close to the handset. He might have been eavesdropping on a conversation. He turned his head Valentino's way. "This thing squawking when you broke in?"

"Squawking?"

"You know, that damn irritating noise it makes when the phone's off the hook and there's nobody on the other end. Ma Bell hates spending her monopoly money on a dial tone."

He hadn't heard anyone but Kyle Broadhead call it Ma Bell in years. Aloud he said, "I can't say for sure. The music was —"

"Yeah." Padilla straightened. "Well, it cuts off after a minute or so." He laid the back of his hand against her bare arm. "Skin's cool. When'd he say he showed up?"

The officer who'd turned off the CD player returned to his notebook. "Two o'clock. The oven started smoking twenty minutes later, he said. Give him five to take the pan out of the oven, fan away the

46

smoke, and bang on the door before he busted it down."

"Make it ten." Valentino rubbed his sore shoulder.

Padilla looked at the watch strapped to his wrist. " 'Kay. We'll see what the rats say, but my guess is her ticker quit before he got here, if what he says checks out. She always sleep in the raw?" he asked Valentino.

He felt himself flush. "I wouldn't know. You've got the wrong idea about our relationship."

"Could be. I'm wrong most of the time. Mickey Mantle struck out more times than he hit. Suppose you give me the right idea."

He told them about their friendship: how it started, why it continued, and why he'd been invited there that day. He started toward the open door, and the package he'd brought and left in the next room, but Padilla barked at him to stay put. "We'll take a look at it back at headquarters after it's dusted, the other one too. Well? Let's have it."

"Have what?"

The lieutenant looked at his cigarette, then parked it behind an ear to dry. "The last time we wanted to take possession of a piece of film, you were all climate-control this and volatile that and vinegar-effect the other thing. I thought I'd let you get it out of your system before I left with the stuff. The brass says we have to start being polite if we don't want go around with cameras stuck on our shirts like the boys on the beat."

"Beata's screen test is of no value to anyone now that she's — gone." Valentino stumbled over the description. "*The Sandpiper* would be no great loss, although of course UCLA would like a shot at acquiring it when you're through with it. We can —"

"Sweet of you." The lieutenant's eyes were bleak, either naturally or from the kind of use to which they'd been put. "How'd she seem lately? Depressed?"

"Anything but. Do you think it's suicide?"

"No. I'm looking for a reason not to rule it out. I don't like that she left dinner in the oven, or that she chose a time when she was entertaining, or that she's naked. The phone in her hand could mean she changed her mind and was trying to call for help when she lost consciousness, but it looks like set dressing to me. You get a feel for these things: when it fell the way it did because it fell the way it did and when somebody got cute and staged it, and this is as phony as a rassling match. I notice when something's there that shouldn't be, also when something that should be there isn't. How about you?"

"I'm still working on that 'when it fell the way it did because it fell the way it did.' " He wondered if they were taught to talk that way when the department hired them or if the department hired them because they talked that way.

Padilla swore, not entirely beneath his breath. "The glass, Buster."

"Valentino. What glass?"

"About time, Mr. Film Detective. No glass."

The drawer of Beata Limerick's drawer was partially open. Padilla grasped hold of the crystal knob and jerked it open the rest of the way. Valentino had noticed something shiny inside earlier, but had refrained from touching the drawer, or anything else in the room. A squat plastic phial like the ones prescription drugs came in rolled to a stop against the front panel. The label, what he could see of it, read NEMBU.

"Nembutal," the lieutenant said. "You can swallow a lethal dose of sleeping pills without water, but I don't know why you'd want to. Why not hang yourself? I mean as long as you're making it uncomfortable."

A flash went off in Valentino's head.

49

"Marilyn Monroe."

"That damn song. I can still hear it too."

"I didn't mean that, although it's significant. The glass isn't the only thing that was missing. I needed the pills to complete the picture and make the connection."

The lieutenant groped for the cigarette behind his ear. "Connect it." He plugged the hole in his mouth.

"The telephone, the nudity, and now the drugs. It matches the situation in Marilyn's bedroom in Brentwood when she was found dead. The coroner blamed it on an overdose of Nembutal. There was no glass there, either. The case was ruled a suicide, but to this day a lot of people are convinced she was murdered."

"I'm sold," Padilla said. "Not on the Monroe case; I was just a gleam in my old man's eye when that one went down, and anyway it's out of my jurisdiction. But Beata? Yeah. It's murder, all right."

6

They went into the living room, where Valentino sank into a chair upholstered in plush pale terry. Beata's decorating tastes had run toward white in every shade available (and a few she'd dreamt up herself and had custom-dyed).

Every *warm* shade, that was. Even her refrigerator and stove could not be referred to as "appliance white." Sleek and modern as it was, her home seemed to envelop all who entered it like a fluffy kitten. The only traces of genuine color in the apartment belonged to the posters and props on display. Padilla, the young officer, and his partner, a weary-looking older man who seemed incapable of speech, remained standing; but their legs were sounder than the film archivist's in the presence of sudden death.

"I heard the Kennedys had Marilyn killed," said the eager youngster. "On account of her relationship with Jack and Bobby."

"Yeah, I'll haul in Caroline for questioning." Padilla's teeth ground at his dead cigarette, glaring at Valentino. "You say this Beata's loaded?"

He hated that term when it was applied to someone he knew; but then, when he considered his life, she'd been the only person he'd known — really known, as opposed to having had contact with — to whom it applied.

"She was one of the richest women in the country." He swept a hand around the apartment, including the panoramic view through the French doors that led to the balcony.

"I'll take your word for it — for now. This town's full of freeloaders eating high on the hog out of somebody else's trough. I carried a spear on the O. J. case; it was rotten with professional houseguests. We'll start there."

"With O. J. Simpson?"

"With money, Hawking. Until it jumps another way I'm working on the assumption some shirttail relative or sponge of a friend stopped her clock for a piece of the inheritance and made it look like it was done by some nutball who saw *Some Like It*

Hot one time too many."

"Gentlemen Prefer Blondes." It came out automatically.

The lieutenant spat out a soggy flake of tobacco, and with it his opinion of the insertion. "I don't go to serial-killer flicks: It means the writers were too lazy to come up with a motive. Unless and until some shrink decides the perp had naughty dreams about Mommy, no cop can make a case."

"But doesn't that fall under the heading of twisting the facts to fit the theory instead of the other way around?"

The lieutenant's beaming face was worse than a scowl.

"Sherlock Holmes. *Those* flicks I go to: His evidence would hold up today. But just now a nutball homicide is the last thing I need. It's been a week since the last one. Call me a cockeyed optimist. I'm going to follow the money, just like Redford and Hoffman, till the trail runs dry; *then* I'll ask around and see what Anthony Hopkins has been up to."

"Congratulations, Lieutenant," Valentino said. "The last time we met, you said you put as many blocks between you and the nearest movie theater as you could."

"I still prefer a good book. It takes time to read, and you get the chance to decide if the guy knows what he's talking about instead of in the car on the way home, fifty bucks to the bad for the price of the gas, parking, ticket, and popcorn. But if you don't keep up with what's in the box office in this town, brother, you're dead."

He took a Ziploc bag out of his pocket. Valentino recognized the note he'd found on the door and had given the young man in uniform: *Let yourself in and sit down on something. I'm putting on my face, and no man should be left to stand that long.* "Would you swear she wrote this?"

"No."

"Yeah?" The cigarette shortened in direct ratio to the motion of his jaws. "Thought you was close."

He didn't like the way Padilla used the word close. It carried all of Kyle Broadhead's innuendo with none of his irony. "Friends, Lieutenant. We didn't exchange love letters, only the occasional e-mail or telephone call. I will say it sounds like her. Anyone who knew her can tell you she was as deprecating to herself as she was to others."

"It says 'Love.' "

"So it does." He wished he smoked, so he could produce an elegant gold-plated case, tap a cigarette on it, and slide it between his lips, like George Sanders in anything. "She was a creature of Hollywood, where it's just another way of signing off. We weren't lovers."

"My job would be a hell of a lot easier if people spoke plain English." He scanned the three lines a second time through the transparent plastic. "I'll give it to the department graphologists. There ought to be samples in the apartment." The note was whisked into a pocket so swiftly Valentino thought he'd actually scored a point. Just when you thought the police an inhuman institution —

Padilla charged on. "Older woman living alone should know better than to leave her door unlocked. Was that normal?"

He smiled through his sadness. He and Beata weren't close, really — not in the sense the lieutenant had suggested, and not in the way Valentino felt toward Kyle Broadhead and Fanta (certainly not like his relationship with Harriet) — but she'd been a bright daub of color in his often-gray academic life.

"I've never heard 'Beata' and 'normal' used in the same sentence. But I wouldn't say she tempted fate. She was superstitious."

"You mean like voodoo, wiccan, shi— stuff like that?" Padilla seemed suddenly to

55

remember the town where he worked.

"Not that extreme. She was a native Californian, she said, and that it was her birthright. She told me she dropped out of the movie business right after Jayne Mansfield died because she believed there was a curse on female blond stars." He began to tick off the names, beginning with Thelma Todd's mysterious death and finishing with the Manson-family bloodbath that had claimed Sharon Tate and a houseful of friends.

" 'The Curse of Marilyn,' seriously?"

"She said so. It was one of the few things she didn't take lightly. Perhaps the only one." *Except friendship,* he thought; but that was one subject he wouldn't open to police cynicism.

"Ironic; I don't think. I wonder who else she told."

"I suppose I'm a suspect."

"That goes with being the one who reported it. You'd be surprised how many cases we nail down *in situ.* If this happened anywhere but this deep in the land of fruits and nuts, I'd book you as a material witness. Where else would two grown people spend a non-smog-alert afternoon indoors in front of a movie screen?"

56

"It's worse than that," Valentino volunteered.

"What could be worse than watching an old movie on a beautiful day?"

"Watching a *bad* old movie."

"That puts you halfway to an insanity plea."

"I don't believe you really think I'm a killer."

Padilla drew out the cigarette, which didn't resemble one anymore, looked around, appeared to think of the CSI team, and put it in a pocket; one could only wonder how many others it had joined there. "Off the record, no. You get a feel for these things — I don't mean that mystical junk, cops are immune to that even in this burg, a hunch is something else — and you aren't putting out anything you didn't last time. That doesn't mean you're home free. I'm wrong most of the time, remember."

Valentino found that less than reassuring; particularly since it was the second time he'd said it.

"Do you think it's likely the note was forged by the murderer?"

"I put 'likely' next to 'luck' in the useful department. But I don't like that a woman who bought into curses and such leaving her door open for just anyone to walk in.

You can spot the local celebrities just by looking for the nearest ring of bodyguards."

"It was different in her day, Lieutenant. The studios controlled the press. Whenever a tabloid got too fresh, its advertisers would mysteriously melt away until it was forced to close. The stars were well-nigh untouchable, therefore more approachable; but people didn't, by and large. They might ask for an autograph, but that was as far as the stalking went. People respected privacy then. Famous actors were like royalty."

"Yeah? Tell that to Buckingham Palace."

"Also she wasn't famous anymore. Not in that sense. A whole generation has grown up since she quit the business."

"I still don't like it, and what I don't like eats my lunch till I see sense in it." He looked at the young officer. "You got his contact info?"

"Yes, sir." He patted his notepad.

"Good. Stay available."

Taking that as a dismissal, Valentino got up.

The older cop took a step and said something low to the lieutenant. It was the first indication the Beverly Hills Police Department hadn't started hiring mutes. *Bashful* was monumental enough.

"Good work." Padilla looked at a set of

58

glass shelves containing Beata's CDs, the boxes lined up neatly in alphabetical order. "Do you know if 'Diamonds Are a Girl's Best Friend' was part of her collection?" he asked Valentino.

"I couldn't say. She usually played classical music when I visited, when she played anything at all."

"We'll check it out. If we don't find the box it belongs to with the others, it means the killer brought it, and that means premeditation."

"How do you poison someone without working it out first?"

"That's up to the medical examiner. Maybe he strangled her or hit her on the head, *then* dressed up the scene to look like something else." His bleak eyes took in the naked corpse. "So to speak."

As Valentino was drawing the door shut behind him, he heard the lieutenant address the older officer. "I wish to hell you'd shut up and let a man think."

7

The crime scene Investigation team was setting up base camp in the lobby as Valentino emerged from the elevator. In their HazMat suits, carrying black steel toolboxes, they resembled the contract laborers who had taken over The Oracle: Both teams were interested primarily in reconstruction, and prepared to destroy everything in their immediate vicinity toward that end. All this took place to the visible consternation of the security guard in the lobby, a retired thirty-year veteran of the California State Police — a hard-boiled force for justice if ever there was one — who'd been tamed by tens of thousands in Christmas gratuities into a glorified house mother. His priorities had shifted from protecting the residents' lives to sequestering them from harsh reality.

"What a shame," Beata had said, "to turn a pit bull into a French poodle."

When Valentino returned to his office, Ruth was absent from her station, sparing him her judgment on how little time he spent there. Perhaps the Call of Nature applied to her as well as to the rest of humanity after all.

He spent much of the next two hours on the telephone, tracking down Beata Limerick's executor according to hints she'd dropped during casual conversation. That party, a Jersey Coaster who seemed to speak entirely through his nose, had heard the news, but from the way he dithered over the dispensation of certain of his late client's estate — *The Sandpiper* being the issue under discussion — Valentino got the impression that some dim future inheritor of his present position might perhaps benefit from the exchange. In a fit of temper he said, "This is trash we're talking about. Ted Turner nailed *Citizen Kane* in thirty minutes."

The supernumerary surprised him with his film scholarship. "Correct me if I'm wrong; but I don't recall either Liz or Dick showing up in that one."

Valentino hit END. He wished he'd called the jerk over a landline so he could slam a receiver into a cradle.

The phone rang immediately. *"What?"* he roared.

"This is Peter." The calmness of the response mortified him. "Your electrician?"

"I'm sorry. I thought you were an executor. Have you fixed the marquee?"

"Well, I'm on track. I think the problem's in the fuse box in the basement."

"There's a fuse box in the basement?"

"My tracking equipment says so. The problem is it's walled up."

He felt a *frisson*. When he'd purchased the property, a walled-up portion of the basement had contained a human skeleton, placed there by the murderer. "Details, please."

"It's not unusual, with buildings this old, that've been redone again and again by this owner and that. In those days, you needed a separate set of fuses for everything: the auditorium, the lobby, the restrooms, the backstage area where they staged live shows before the feature. It was a real drain. So what I need to do is punch a hole in the south wall of the basement, see can I track down the box that operates the marquee and fix it."

Valentino subsided in his chair, seeing dollar bills flying out the window on wings. "What's that going to cost?"

"Let me see." Something clattered on the other end of the line: a calculator. Shift the image from dollar bills to fives, then tens. Twenties, by the bale? Ulysses S. Grant was fast becoming his least favorite president.

"Fifty should do it."

"Dollars?" He couldn't remember the last time he'd heard that denomination spoken aloud. Pocket change.

"Maybe less. What we do, we drill a small hole, stick a teeny camera through it on a stick. If a fuse box shows up, we bust through. Then we identify the burned-out fuse, screw in a fifty-cent replacement, and we're good to go. Easy cheesy, Japanesy, as my old man used to say. I guess he'd have to say 'Asian' now, but it wouldn't be as much fun."

"God bless your old man."

"I said *if.* We don't find a box, it's a whole new ball game."

He couldn't think of anything else to say. "Play ball."

The ill wind blew him some good. Two lines in the *L.A. Times* identified Valentino as the man who'd discovered the murdered woman, and the owner of a string of auto dealerships in the Valley read them and called with an offer.

"Free lubes for life?" asked Broadhead, when Valentino burst into his office with the news.

"Even better."

"Better than never having to pay for an oil change again? This should be good." The professor drummed together a sheaf of closely printed pages, made sure all the edges were flush, and dumped it into his wastebasket. His colleague wondered often about the contents of his trash. Just how many unique gems of cinema history routinely went up in the incinerator kept the younger man awake nights.

"It is. His great-great-grandfather was a mechanic with Hal Roach Studios."

"Is that all? *My* great-great-grandfather tried to blow up Czar Nicholas the First."

"Be serious for just a minute."

"I'm always serious. What's funny about attempted regicide? Had he succeeded, there never would have been a Nicholas the Second, and what would have happened to the Russian revolution? McDonald's would be serving beluga at the drive-through."

"*This* mechanic," the other plowed on, "maintained the junk Model T's Roach bought for a buck apiece and systematically destroyed during his comedy shorts. When the dealer read what I do for a living he asked if I'd be interested in taking some material off his hands. He knows nothing about the movies, but his father left him a dozen cans of film and he's kept them in storage for forty years, not knowing what else to do with them. If what he says holds any water, he's sitting on a cache of silent Laurel and Hardy shorts that haven't seen the sun since the premiere of *The Jazz Singer.*"

"What shape are they in?"

"Round, and about so deep." He spread his hands like a man boasting about a fish.

Broadhead scowled. "Never rub another man's rhubarb, boy. What's he asking?"

" 'When can you come and get them out of my basement? My wife wants to install a ballet barre.' "

The two men who comprised the backbone of the Film Preservation Department invested two days in examining the loot, which turned out to be a mixed bag, in varying degrees of condition, of outtakes, finished footage, and thirty-seven feet of Billy Gilbert sneezing; not quite the treasure trove they'd hoped for, but an advance of one-tenth of one percent against the ninety percent of pre-talkies that had been sacrificed to time and complacency. The auto dealer, many times a millionaire, refused monetary compensation, but agreed to a line in the credits of the restored films honoring the contribution of Clarence "Crankcase" Mooney, his great-great-grandfather.

The dean of their program turned out to be a Billy Gilbert fan. ("Who knew?" Broadhead said. "He hasn't cracked a smile since Mount St. Helens.") He went to the board of regents and arranged a substantial bonus for the professor and his protégé. Broadhead used his to upgrade Fanta's arrangements for their wedding. Valentino spent his on gold leaf. For the first time since President Truman, the banister of the grand staircase to The Oracle's mezzanine glittered as if wired for electric light.

He was glad something did. So far the electrician had bored more holes than a colony of worms and his fiber-optic camera hadn't discovered anything resembling an auxiliary fuse box.

Then came an envelope addressed to the film archivist by a former bridge partner of Beata Limerick's, inviting him to attend her memorial service.

Cars were parked on both sides of the street for blocks; Beata had been no recluse, with many friends and, Valentino assumed, still a respectable number of fans. He left his beat-up compact a stone's throw from Griffith Park and walked with Harriet along the sidewalk leading to the colonnaded front of the Mormon temple. A leather sole scraped concrete behind him and Kyle Broadhead came abreast of the couple.

He showed them his invitation. "Beata a Latter-Day Saint," he said. "I had her down as a Unitarian; one of those useful denominations that lets you appear to be a believer without actually praying."

"She never mentioned religion, and I never saw anything faith-related in her apartment. She was a private person when all was said and done."

"With good reason. No studio would have touched her if it got out she wasn't a conventional Christian."

"That may have been necessary when she was acting, but when I knew her she didn't behave as if she had any secrets, dark or otherwise."

"I didn't know her as well as you did, but she had both."

"How can you be so sure?"

"Because people who don't have something to hide bore me sick."

Valentino changed the subject. "Where's Fanta?"

"Attending a lecture on tarts. She sends

67

regrets."

"You mean torts," Harriet said.

"No, the city council's debating a measure to shift prostitution enforcement from the pros to the johns. Her faculty advisor told her to brush up. Speaking of enforcers, have you heard anything from the Gay Lieutenant?"

"What makes you think Padilla's — ? Oh. You were being ironic. Not a word, and there's been nothing new in the media. Maybe she died of natural causes after all."

"One can only hope. Just when it seems the world's laid this Marilyn thing to rest, something else comes along to stir it back up. Monroe's real tragedy was that being a movie star wasn't good enough for her: She had to be an actress, too. So she went to that New York School crowd and they stamped out what genuine talent she had."

Just then a nondescript car pulled up in front of the entrance and an LAPD officer in uniform got out to open the door on the passenger's side for his superior. As before, the Homicide lieutenant's gray suit seemed to be wearing him rather than the other way around.

"Maybe he came to pay his respects," Valentino said.

"Maybe," said Broadhead. "Or maybe he's

been on grave detail so long he's taken up funeral-going as a hobby."

Harriet squeezed Valentino's hand: a gesture of support as well as confirmation that like it or not Ray Padilla was there to do his job.

8

The man from Homicide trotted up the steps to the entrance without glancing Valentino's way, but the archivist was sure he'd seen him. He'd spent enough time around experienced detectives to know they had the peripheral vision of a chameleon.

It was a heartbreakingly bright afternoon, with the Ozone Alert at zero and the sun pasted on a Crayola-blue sky: Paint a smile on its face and it might have been drawn by a child.

The cheery weather depressed him even more than the event itself. He preferred gray overcast and a weepy rain during funerary events, sparing him pity for the deceased, who at least had not missed a beautiful day. The crowd filled all the chairs and stood along the walls, while security men in black double-knit suits kept photographers and camera crews from entering the temple. The theme from *A Summer Place* was playing over the sound system: the deceased's plucky sense of humor personified. Sandra Dee had beaten her out for the role of the daughter, and been stereotyped as the Troubled Blonde for the rest of her career.

There was no casket. The body had yet to be released by the coroner. An enormous color blowup of the guest of honor late in life beamed out from an easel on the dais at the front of the room, perfectly coiffed with tiny tasteful diamonds in her lobes.

After some searching, they found three seats together, and browsed the pamphlet they'd each been handed by an attendant at the door. Beata smiled on the cover, this time in the full bloom of youth, costumed as an Egyptian dancer complete with golden-snake headband and exotic eye shadow. Beneath the photograph, in skirling italics, was the line:

Excuse my dust.
— Dorothy Parker

Valentino chuckled despite himself. Inside, where there was usually a text with quotations from poetry or scripture, a collage of photos spread across two pages: a sepia-tone studio shot of an adorable golden-ringleted toddler, a stunning twentysomething sipping a Manhattan across a nightclub table from silver-templed Clark Gable, a cheese-cake snap of a teen beauty queen in white shorts and a halter top, a wedding-anniversary portrait showing a ruddy senior citizen cheek-to-cheek with a radiantly smiling wife a fraction of his age (photographic proof, for Valentino, that her marriage had been no sham); others, each selected to harvest smiles rather than tears.

"I'm sure she planned this," Valentino told Broadhead.

"So have I. I'm to be thrown in the recycling bin, and reincarnated as the soap in Sophia Loren's shower."

Harriet, seated at Valentino's right, nudged him with her elbow, stopping him in mid-sigh. He wondered just what sort of occasion it would take to quell the professor's relentless cynicism.

Someone tapped him on the shoulder. He twisted in his seat to face Ray Padilla. Like the proverbial stopped clock that was right twice a day, the lieutenant's perennially grim demeanor fit the present proceedings. "If I were half the people here, I'd think twice before going to a funeral. The ushers might not let them leave."

The film archivist surveyed the sea of white heads. "Thirty years ago, you'd have had to pay admission to see them. You don't often find this much Hollywood history gathered in one spot."

"Thirty years ago they'd all have been suspects. I don't see a set of muscles strong enough to force those pills down even an old woman's throat."

"Was it the pills that killed her?"

"M.E. says yes. She put up a fight; lesions and contusions and a fractured skull, all artfully concealed by someone who knew something about hairdressing and makeup. The deeper we dig, the more this looks like an industry job."

An elderly man Valentino recognized vaguely from a failed '70s sitcom coughed pointedly into a crepey fist. Padilla, who was sitting next to him, looked at Valentino and jerked his head toward the back of the room. Valentino patted Harriet's hand, fumbled his way past fellow mourners to the aisle, and joined the lieutenant in a corner behind a potted bougainvillea.

"No other Marilyn CDs on the premises," Padilla said. "No box for the one that was playing. No prints we can't account for either, surprise-surprise. Like anybody clever enough to dress up the scene wouldn't think to wear gloves. And our graphology guy says that wasn't her handwriting on the note."

"What about the Kennedys?"

Bleak eyes stared without expression. "We don't rule anything out. Caroline was in New York, giving an endorsement speech for a Democratic candidate for mayor and the rest of the brood was split up between the family compound in Massachusetts and Switzerland: Skiing. Some people never learn."

"If you told them that, I wish I'd been listening on the extension."

"I never figured to make captain anyway. Too many press conferences. You probably guessed I don't test high on patience and diplomacy. But I'm not here about the Limerick woman."

"You're not? I thought it was standard operating procedure, in case the murderer shows up for the service."

"That's somebody else's duty. I've cracked a dozen homicides and not once did the one we nailed come to pay respects. It was the same thing when I was with Arson, but I went to more fires than Smokey Bear on the slim-to-nothing chance the perp hung around to drool over the flames."

"You just trashed half the crime movies I've seen."

"Well, keep it under your hat. The more

guff gets out there, the better for us: Like that malarkey about a cop having to tell you he's a cop if you ask or he can't arrest you."

"I knew that one. Lieutenant, am I still a suspect?"

"I wouldn't brag about it. It isn't exactly an exclusive club. I talked to an elder," he added.

The abrupt change of subject caught him off-balance. He wondered if it was some new interrogative tactic. "An elder what?"

"Mormon muckety-muck; that's him, the bird in the black double-knit pretending to arrange the flowers. He's counting the house. The Limerick woman was a good, God-fearing woman, according to him. She told him she was leaving ten percent of her estate to the church."

"She never did anything halfway."

"Something we've got in common. Now I get to add most of the population of the State of Utah to the list of suspects. Feeling a little less special?"

An unearthly squeal split the air. The man Padilla had identified as an elder was adjusting the microphone on the dais. The service was about to begin.

"Since I'm no longer Public Enemy Number One, may I return to my seat?"

"In a minute. Where were you last night

75

between ten P.M. and midnight?"

Valentino, who always broke out in sweats when pressed by authority, reached back to peel his suitcoat and shirt away from his back. It had turned clammy. He'd heard some version of that question on the soundtracks of countless melodramas, never expecting he'd have to answer it himself.

"What happened last night?"

"See, it works like this: *I* ask the questions, you blurt out the first lie that comes into your head, I keep asking till you stumble over the truth."

"I resent that."

"What'd I say about patience and diplomacy? You want me to repeat the question, like in court?"

"I was at home, going over construction bills."

"Anyone who can verify that?"

"A plumber in Tarzana, though he might not admit it. I called him at his home around eleven to ask why it cost six hundred dollars to unplug a drain in the ladies' room."

"You better hope he isn't dead, too. Landline?"

"Yes."

"We'll check out the phone company records."

"What's so important about where I was last night?"

"Did you know a woman named Karen Ogilvie?"

The chill spread to Valentino's face. "I know her husband, Morris. He's a major contributor to the Film Preservation Department. Karen used to do television, a long time ago; she was Karen Earl then. She quit acting when she married Morris. Has something happened to her?"

He'd raised his voice a notch. A woman with blue-rinsed hair and a flesh-colored button in each ear turned around in her back-row seat and shushed him. He'd seen her face, unwrinkled then but crowned by the same beehive, belonging to a Twist-dancer in a 1960s teen flick.

Padilla, staring at her, made a circular motion with his hand. She blew a gust of air and faced front. But he lowered his voice. "Palm Springs PD faxed these over this morning." He slid a manila envelope from his jacket, tipped out the contents, and passed them to Valentino.

"Dear friends," intoned the elder at the front of the room, "thank you for attending this celebration of the life of Beata Limerick, our sister in faith."

Studying the pictures he'd been handed,

Valentino tuned out the eulogy. They were smudged and grainy, printed on coarse non-reflective paper, but the face of the dead woman — for she was emphatically dead — struck a chord in his memory. Oddly, although he'd known her in old age, his first image was of a breathtaking blond siren first encountered on a fluttery old-fashioned picture tube early in his puberty. He blinked, bringing the visible tracks of time back into focus.

Karen Earl Ogilvie was slumped over a steering wheel with her hair disarranged and dark smears on her forehead, chin, and the collar of her fur coat. Her eyes were open, her lips slightly parted as if to ask the photographer to wait while she freshened her lipstick. The fuzzy quality, reproduced in black-and-white from what had probably been a color original, put him in mind of freeze-frames from a 1930s newsreel com-memorating some sensational tragedy; cruel, uncompromising, and somehow more sordid than anything he'd seen in a voyeuris-tic cable reality show. He experienced a thrill of déjà vu; double-whammy, as it came with that same sense of something lurking inches outside the reach of his memory that had visited him in the bedroom where Beata died.

Padilla took back the material and slid it into its envelope. "She dined out with girlfriends last night. Husband was in Chicago on business, that's confirmed. When the maid came in at seven A.M., she heard a motor running and looked in the garage. It was still running when the first officer responded, on about a teaspoon of gas left in the tank."

"Carbon monoxide?"

"Toxicology team's testing, but the results won't change anything. That's blood on her face and coat. Her Porsche was undamaged, so she wasn't in an accident. Someone cracked her a couple of times with what we used to call a blunt instrument. There's a scientific word, but I stopped listening to the eggheads when they invented DNA. I need it in my job like a monkey needs a top hat. Palm Springs cops think the killer was waiting for her in the garage, which meant he had access, and probably to the house as well."

"You're certain it was a he?"

"He, she, it; who are you, Gloria Steinem? You don't have to be the Hulk to swing a club. But you, pal, know two murder victims spaced three days apart, so here I am."

"Did Ogilvie tell you he knows me?"

"We missed him in Chicago. He's in the

air, on his way back to a surprise. They make you turn off your phone when you take off."

"... a woman of insight and dedication to the church ..." said the elder.

"Is it against the law to know people?" Valentino raised his voice again, and got a chorus of geriatric hissing for the indiscretion.

"I'm not finished. Mrs. Ogilvie wasn't wearing the same clothes she'd had on when she left her friends. They said she was wearing a two-piece suit and no coat. Maid says the coat was hers, but she hadn't worn it in years, on account of all those animal-rights people slinging around buckets of red paint; kept it in a storage bag in a cedar closet. The lab rats are pretty sure someone put her in a dress after death. They found the suit crammed in a hamper. The extra flourishes made me think of Beata Limerick, and Beata Limerick made me think of you."

The lieutenant refolded the envelope lengthwise and returned it to his pocket. "Luck, that's the job sometimes: You close your eyes and pin the tail on the donkey's keister right off the bat."

I know the feeling. Aloud, Valentino said: "If the murderer changed her clothes after he killed her, how did blood get on the collar of the coat?"

"It wasn't a spill, it was a smear. Pattern's different. Maybe he got blood on him and used the coat to wipe it off."

"Unless he did it deliberately."

"Why would he do that?"

"Why would he change her clothes?"

Padilla pursed his lips, turning his mournful face into a sour apple. "There's more."

"Isn't there always?" He was anxious to be dismissed. Missing Beata's service would be the rudest thing he could do to a friend.

Unless he solved her murder. That would wipe out the offense.

The lieutenant ignored the question. "The side door to the garage was bolted from the house side. That means our friend let himself out that way, but we can't figure out why he bothered to bolt the door behind him.

"I'm not coming to you just because you could be a person of interest," he went on. "We don't get many flat-out murder mysteries. Most times we find the perp in the same room with the victim, literally red-handed and ready to spill his guts. This one has all the earmarks of those screwy whodunits you're always going on about. I know some guys in the department who moonlight as technical advisors on movie sets, showing

John Travolta how to walk like a cop instead of an East L.A. gigolo. So I'm suggesting you return the favor and be a technical advisor to the police, only you don't get paid, just the satisfaction of contributing to your community and also maybe get a break if you know more about this mess than you're letting on. You saw the Marilyn connection last time. See anything like that here?"

In a flash, Valentino crossed the narrow chasm that had separated him from something remembered. No wonder his mind had leapt to Depression-era newsreels: Details of the story had blazed through glossy picture palaces and dusty small-town theaters for weeks; culminating, as unsolved puzzles always did, in shrugs, then the next item of juicy gossip.

"The dress she had on," he said.

"Yeah?"

"Was it blue?"

9

"Thelma Todd," Valentino said, when the color of the dead woman's dress was confirmed.

"Esther McGillicuddy," Padilla said. "I can call out women's names at random too."

"The movie star."

"Of course."

"You never heard of her, right?"

"I never heard of the fifth Beatle, but I know you can't finish a sentence without a movie star's name in it."

"It will save us both a lot of time if we can continue this conversation at my place. Right now I'd like to say good-bye to an old friend."

Something stirred behind the Reaperesque face. The film archivist couldn't quite extend himself far enough to believe the man was capable of sympathy; but he looked at his wristwatch. "I'll meet you at that waxworks you call home sweet home in an hour."

He drove Harriet to her apartment, but she stopped him before he could get out to see her to the door. Her expression made up for all the human emotion the lieutenant seemed to have been born without. "Are you sure you don't want me to go with you? I'm with the department too, remember. I know enough of the tricks of intimidation to head him off."

"I'm starting to be an expert myself." He kissed her. She responded with more feeling than usual.

The unmarked car was parked next to the fire hydrant in front of The Oracle, with the same uniformed officer seated behind the wheel. Padilla was smoking a cigarette under the marquee, which wore a polystyrene bag to protect the exposed wires from the elements. Valentino couldn't remember the last time he'd seen the lieutenant actually set fire to one of his coffin nails. They shook hands — much to the host's surprise — and entered the lobby.

"Looks like the same train wreck to me," Padilla said, crushing out his smoke on a patch of bare plywood. "They built the pyramids in less time."

"They had slave labor. I'm paying time-and-a-half for overtime."

The room was a shambles of coiled wire, piled plaster, and tarpaulins hanging from scaffolds. The crew was eating lunch, dropping mustard and pickles on porous marble.

"Actually," Valentino added, "there's been quite a bit of progress, most of it beneath the surface."

"That's what my mother-in-law said about her colon flush. Staircase looks good."

"I've got Billy Gilbert to thank for that."

"He does nice work. What's so delicate we couldn't talk about it in front of a bunch of Mormons? You got the home-court advantage: Run with it."

For answer, Valentino led the way into the auditorium, where the seats that had been reupholstered wore protective covers and the ones that hadn't lay about in every stage of dismantlement. He opened a door hidden behind fresh molding and they climbed the steep unfinished stairs to the projection booth. There, a rollaway bed and a camp refrigerator shared quarters with great twin Bell & Howell projectors, racks and stacks of DVDs, videotapes, and cans of film, and Valentino's literature on the history of motion pictures, temporarily housed in plastic orange crates. A square opening looked out on the screen in the proscenium arch down-stairs, furled like a ship's mainsail.

Padilla pointed at the projectors. "Why two? You can barely turn around in here without triggering the Big One."

"Three-D, old-school. The trick is to co-ordinate the frames so the audience isn't seeing two Ray Millands at once in *Dial M for Murder.* That takes a specialist, and they don't come cheap."

"What is it with you and murder? *I* have to work with it, but *you* don't."

"My corpses are tidier, courtesy of the Motion Picture Code." He slid a tattered paperback from one of the crates. "Thelma Todd was before your time. Mine, too. She was a glamour queen and a gifted comedi-enne, like Carole Lombard; who was an-other doomed blonde for Beata's curse."

"You'd think they'd learn to lay off the peroxide." Padilla looked around, as if the carnage of the theater under constant renovation held more interest for him than murders ancient and current. "How do you live like this?"

"You know the housing situation. I went apartment hunting and wound up in a gilt palace, minus most of the gilt. They'd have torn it down by now if I hadn't bought it."

"So far you're not selling me on why you did."

He cleared his throat; reminding himself once again that preaching to the unconverted was an uphill climb. He handed over the open book. " 'Hot Toddy,' they called her."

His guest studied the glossy black-and-white photograph of a beautiful woman with curly blond hair, huge eyes, and a pert, pointed chin. Plainly the flat colorless eyes were committing every detail to memory. At length he flicked his fingers at the page.

"I saw something about this surfing channels on TV. It had that dame in it from *WKRP in Cincinnati.* It stalled me for a good minute and a half."

"I know the one you mean: A quickie starring Loni Anderson, a forty-odd sitcom star playing an actress who was murdered in her twenties."

"Yeah, well, they all looked older back then. All them martinis and Luckies." Padilla dealt himself another cigarette.

Valentino found the chapter he wanted. "Todd was a terrific actress with great comic timing, but her life was a mess off-screen, even for a star of her era. She had an affair with Lucky Luciano. The gangster?"

"Him I know. I guess that's before the glitter gang started hanging out with basketball players." He scanned the rows of titles: *Fade to Black, A Cast of Killers, Hollywood Babylon.* "You got yourself quite a mug file here. All these people have a screw loose?"

"Most were levelheaded, some merely eccentric. It's the notorious ones that give a place a bad reputation. In those days L.A. was the last western boomtown, with everything that entails. Throw a lot of young undereducated people into a pile of money, cover them with the kind of adoration normally reserved for saints, and anything can happen."

"Not much has changed from where I sit. We got an entire evidence room reserved for celebrity sex tapes, just in case something comes under our jurisdiction."

Valentino hesitated to heap more fuel on the lieutenant's blazing disdain for the industry that gave him his livelihood; but the thought of a homicidal maniac cutting a bloody swath through his friends got the better of his pride. "You're aware Luciano's relationship with women got him deported to Italy."

"He was a pimp. Toddy turned tricks for him, that it?"

He'd feared just that reaction. Whenever

88

someone pricked the Dream Factory, Valentino bled. "No one knows, that's the point. In 1935 her maid found her in her garage, slumped over the wheel of her Packard convertible. The ignition was on, there was blood on her face and fur coat, the door to the garage was barred on the other side."

"Huh."

"The coroner ruled death by monoxide poisoning. She was still wearing her rings and a diamond necklace, so robbery was eliminated as a motive." He looked up from the page. "She had on a blue dress under the coat."

"So you figure we got us a copycat who knows his Tinseltown trivia."

"Maybe he's read this book." The film archivist closed it and showed Padilla the cover. It was titled *Hollywood's Unsolved Mysteries.* He offered it to the lieutenant.

Padilla kept his hands in his pockets. "Maybe he has. Maybe he knows it by heart." Padilla looked at him, his eyes as flat as bottle caps.

"I just talked myself to the top of your list, didn't I?" Valentino lowered the book.

The other returned his gaze to the library. "It's a long list, but unless the Earl-Ogilvie woman was a Mormon maybe I won't have to take a trip to Salt Lake City; that's if this isn't a coincidence and we're not looking at two different killers. I hope for your sake your alibi floats. You're the suspect every junior detective dreams of."

Valentino returned the paperback to its space. "You'll need a motive. I liked Beata, and apart from a brush or two when dealing with her husband I never saw Karen Earl outside episodes of the original *Untouchables* and *Peter Gunn.*"

"I told you what's happened to motive. It's not just serial nuts: Guy cuts you off in traffic, looks sideways at your date, wears glasses that remind you of your crummy old man, he's toast. Just last week I got a confession out of a fifteen-year-old kid that shot up a Burger King because a girl told him on Facebook she was too busy washing her hair to watch him shoot rats down by the docks. She'd never even been to the restaurant. These days, all you need is an Arab clerk who shortchanges you to take it out on the first man you see wearing a turban."

"I think there's more to it than that, Lieutenant."

The other man found a flake of cigarette ash on his prison of a suit and flicked it to the floor with a savage movement, as if it were some kind of loathsome insect. "Don't start that Curse of Marilyn stuff again. Press gets wind of it, I'll be shaking crank tipsters off my lapels, and then the chief's going to start shopping for smartypants psychics: Before you know it I'm wearing pansy makeup on *Inside Edition.* You know what I think? I think our friend's counting on that to throw us off the trail. He's got a certain victim in mind, and he's out to cover up the why under a load of corpses. The hard part's going to be nailing him before he piles up too many."

He couldn't help asking. "How many is too many?"

"Brother, he's already caught more than his limit."

10

Throughout the next week, Valentino drew all his information on the murders from *ET, Access Hollywood, Variety,* and the *Times.* A succession of talking heads plastered with bronzers, blush, and hairspray to King Tut-like preservation, doddering Distinguished Columnists, and breathless sidewalk correspondents with microphones lapped up the details like alcoholics at an open bar, but made no attempt to link the slayings to the suspicious deaths of Marilyn Monroe and Thelma Todd. Each time Valentino checked in, he held his breath, but after a dozen news cycles had come and gone without including a lesson in local lore, he gave up waiting for the other shoe to drop: Padilla and the LAPD appeared to have had some influence on such speculation, either through intimidation or barter; but fresh facts did surface.

Karen Ogilvie had whiled away the afternoon before her dinner out with friends screening old footage in her home theater, a staple in the motion-picture community every bit as crucial as swimming pools and tennis courts. She was featured in every film: Inevitably, comparisons were made with Gloria Swanson as Norma Desmond, the has-been haunted silent siren of *Sunset Boulevard;* missing entirely the more direct connection to the near-forgotten Todd. Notwithstanding that omission, the employees in Research had little difficulty in dredging up art on the victim of the month: One of Karen's old commercials was repeated so often, Spic and Span later reported its best quarter in a decade.

Beata wasn't neglected. Metrocolor newsreels, shot to cut the studio's losses after her desertion, trumpeted the "recently retired starlet's" Cinderella-like wedding to a silver-haired billionaire industrialist, complete with confetti and streamers flying from the SS *United States* and the happy couple waving to well-wishers on shore. Watching the clips, Valentino's eyes grew misty: It was clear from the lovely young bride's smile (as it had been in her memorial pamphlet) that she was in love with her husband. She'd seldom mentioned him when they'd spoken, and he'd always assumed that her interest in him had been purely financial; now he realized that the subject of his passing was too painful for her to discuss. He'd known so little about her, and felt that he'd been less than a true friend because of his lack of interest beyond her connection with old Hollywood. Her career had been but a brief moment in a rich life.

No public connection was made with the two deaths, apart from their close proximity; the LAPD had been adept in connecting Ogilvie's fate to probable suicide.

To his relief, the reports made no mention of the archivist, but Lieutenant Padilla put in an appearance (determinedly without powder or paint), informing press-conference attendees that whoever had killed Beata was probably known to and trusted by her, in order to have obtained entry to her homes and proximity to her person.

"You mean like the Boston Strangler?" offered one plucky young thing who seemed to want to break out of the red-carpet ghetto into serious journalism. (Her sharp eyes suggested suspicion that Beata's was not an isolated case.)

"She wasn't strangled." This non sequitur was as tidy a diversion as could be imagined.

For all his talk of avoiding the spotlight, the lieutenant was as adept at handling the press as any department spokesman.

Just in case Valentino might feel he was off the hook, Padilla called him twice, ostensibly to ask questions he'd neglected earlier, but quite obviously to remind him he was still of central interest to the investigation. That was another of his manipulative skills, never allowing a suspect a moment of complacency.

Despite all official efforts at stirring up dust, conspiracy theorists burned up the Internet with the speculation that a serial killer was targeting old-time actresses. The buzz drove every other subject off the front page and past the first commercial spot:

A quake in San Bernardino measuring 3.2 on the Richter scale aired for thirty seconds. No one was injured, and the damage was minimal, but at any other time, all the local stations would be trotting out pet geologists with their doomsday charts.

A mayor in the wine country sent a revealing selfie to his secretary's phone; the story blew over before he could face more cameras with his wife by his side (and he was a Republican, thus fair game);

An '80s TV hunk, growing a little seedy around the edges but still fodder for rumors about his swinging sex life, came out of the closet, almost without notice;

Geoffrey Root, a popular female impersonator who played local nightclubs, was killed in an automobile accident. Under normal circumstances his high visibility, skewering (and sometimes amusing) such flashy femmes as Dolly Parton, Zsa Zsa Gabor, Cher, and Madonna with his dead-on impressions in sequins and heavy makeup, would have led off every broadcast. Instead, the tragic on-site footage of shorn metal and scattered personal possessions was sandwiched between the latest unilluminating report on the murder(s?) and a puff-piece on Jennifer Lopez.

Valentino, who'd had his fill of sudden death, would have switched off the TV in his office if both hands weren't occupied spooling frames of a Betty Boop cartoon on his Moviola; but when the camera panned to the accordioned hood of Root's mint-condition 1966 Buick and what lay upon it, all the blood dumped out of the film archivist's face. He muted the sound and reached for his telephone. It rang before he could punch the first button.

"I was just about to call you," he said.

Padilla said, "Yeah, I'm watching it, too."

In a flash, Valentino knew they'd both

made the same connection; but the lieutenant pushed on before the other could interject anything.

"It should tickle you to know you're no longer my primary in the Ogilvie case. Your electrician backed up your story. Sometimes it pays to be cheap enough to call a guy up and complain about a bill after business hours."

"Thanks. What do you know about the Root accident?"

"I just heard about it, same as you. It's CHiP's baby, but I got eyes, and you can't beat HDTV for clear reception. Hang on."

A frustrated Valentino listened to soothing soft '70s rock for ten solid minutes. In spite of himself, he was humming "Rocket Man" when the music stopped.

"I just got off the horn with Laurel Canyon," Padilla said. "Jogger found Root's heap folded up against a tree there around sunup. Looks like he lost control on a curve, busted through a guardrail, and did the bank shot down a ravine. The place is rotten with 'em; troopers peel some kid off a cottonwood or a Douglas fir every prom night. If Root wasn't in show business he'd never have made the six o'clock report."

"What I —"

"I'm coming to it. He wasn't wearing a

seat belt. His head punched a hole in the windshield." Something rustled dryly: Was Padilla chuckling? One of Valentino's greatest fears was he'd become so familiar with mayhem he, too, would find it something to laugh about. "Root was headed to a charity benefit, which was canceled when he didn't turn up; had a bunch of costumes in the car: Left a trail of pink feather boas and rhinestones all down the ravine. First responders said it looked like J. Edgar Hoover's spring cleaning."

"Lieutenant, that's ghastly."

"You're telling me. He showed up at the morgue in black patent-leather pants and a white angora sweater. I didn't think they went."

"That's not what I meant; but I'm less concerned about his costume than I am about his wig."

"Which one? There was enough fake hair on those rocks to knit a gorilla suit."

He swallowed his resentment over this latest example of police torture, assuming an air of patience. "If you called me for the same reason I was about to call you, I think you know which wig I'm talking about."

A short silence crackled, during which Padilla seemed to have found a shred of compassion and poked it into an envelope reserved for evidence. In any case when he came back on he sounded like a person. "You're not the only one who can read a book about old movie queens. I've been boning up since we talked. Where are you?"

"At work."

"It's after seven. If I sank as much as you did into where I lived, I'd spend a lot more time there."

"I have to spend as much time here as I do in order to be able to sink that much into where I live."

"I'll send a car."

■ ■ ■ ■

II
THE GIRL CAN'T
HELP IT

■ ■ ■ ■

11

"There's a cop here for you."

One of the disadvantages of working with a fellow workaholic like Ruth was — well, she was always *there.* Her presence could especially be depended upon when the opportunity presented itself to heap humiliation on a superior; particularly Valentino, whose function to the university she regarded as less respectable than that of the man who filled the vending machines in the student union.

For once he decided to go on the offensive; something Kyle Broadhead did routinely and without hesitation.

"I knew they'd catch up with me one day," he said into the intercom. "Ruth, I've been robbing the place blind for years. You'll find my stash in the ceiling."

"Which ceiling? There are eight in this building alone."

"I can never remember." Five minutes

later, seated beside the officer Padilla had sent for him, he pictured the old gargoyle hurrying out to fetch a crowbar.

Immediately he felt guilty; something Kyle Broadhead never did, routinely or otherwise.

Police stations invariably disappointed the film archivist; they bore little resemblance to the romantically grubby wainscoted rooms walled with battered file cabinets and carpeted with squashed cigarette butts he knew from countless Warner Brothers features. The Beverly Hills station, well-ventilated, brightly lit, and cut up into cubicles, was no exception. It might have belonged to an accounting firm in Fresno, or some place equally prosaic. Except for the odd exposed service automatic in a tan belt holster (and even those were no longer exclusive to law-enforcement professionals), the men and women fingering the keyboards of computers and sprinting to and from a community printer were indistinguishable from the common office drone, and the desks themselves were decorated with family pictures instead of the Ten Most Wanted.

But Ray Padilla's private office (semi-private, actually; the glass-paneled walls fell two feet short of the ceiling) comforted the visitor. Something about the long-expired African violet and tasteful prints left to hang at Krazy Kat angles on the walls suggested they'd been inherited from a previous tenant, and his successor hadn't bothered to replace them with something better suited to his personality. It was a place of work exclusively, and the suggestion that the occupant refused to expose anything from his private life to its sinister confines restored hope in his humanity.

He was in shirtsleeves with the cuffs turned back, no tie. Shedding departmental conservatism seemed to have had a softening effect. Once again he shook hands, and waved Valentino into an orange plastic scoop chair facing a heap of papers theoretically supported by a desk.

"My first partner worked the Jayne Mansfield case from this end," he said. "Kept bending my year about it till he retired. Jayne was running around with a mob lawyer at the time, name of Brody. He represented Jack Ruby, the guy that shot Lee Harvey Oswald. What is it with these sex kittens and gangsters?"

"Politicians, too," Valentino said. "Don't forget politicians."

"Don't waste your breath. Can't be done. Anyway she, Brody, and her teenage son were killed in June 'sixty-seven when her Buick rear-ended a truck on I-90 in Louisiana, on their way to do a TV interview in New Orleans. I caught a sergeant there in R-and-I just before quitting, Central Standard Time."

Without warning, he swiveled his computer screen to face his guest. A fuzzy black-and-white photo taken at the nearly fifty-year-old crime scene leapt out at him in grisly detail. As many times as he'd come across pictures of the tragedy, this was his first exposure to one too graphic to release to the press. He turned his eyes away from the mangled remains of the 1960s' most famous sex symbol being loaded into a polystyrene bag.

"You can see she wasn't decapitated, in spite of all the rumors; not that pushing your face through a windshield at the rate of seventy miles an hour won't do the job just as thorough. What happened, the wig she had on flew out through the broken glass and landed on the hood and a gawker saw it and jumped to the most sensational conclusion; as gawkers will, especially when a movie star's involved and they can sell the story to the tabloids. That's it there."

He pointed, but Valentino kept his face averted. He'd seen it perched obscenely on the Buick's corrugated hood; the same cotton-candy wig Beata Limerick had displayed so proudly in a glass case in her living room. Frivolous vanity item that it was, in that context it was nearly as grotesque as the storied severed head.

"No *in situ* pictures from California Highway Patrol yet," Padilla went on. "From what I got from the sergeant on his way out the door, the scene's a pretty close reconstruction."

"Coincidence?"

"They happen, believe me. If those movie cops you spend so much time looking at were for real, they'd've come across them often enough not to blow 'em off the way they do. But hang on." He swung the monitor back his way, rattled some keys, and slid a mouse on a pad advertising a local funeral home. Something about the movement put Valentino in mind of someone working the pointer on a Ouija board.

Padilla grunted and rotated the screen again. "These Sacramento boys run an efficient operation. They got Geoffrey Root's portfolio off his website and gave me the link. Take a look."

He was almost afraid to for fear of another nightmare image to take to bed, but he found himself looking at a grid of photos that made him think of the opening credits to *Brady Bunch* reruns. At first he thought that nine different women were smiling at him from publicity mug shots, but on closer examination spotted similarities in the features. They were all one woman — or rather, it dawned on him then, one *man,* sporting different female hairstyles and makeup.

The female impersonator was an artist, that much was clear; one who used himself as a canvas. To the unindoctrinated, the electronic album showcased Mae West in her prime, Elizabeth Taylor as Cleopatra, Streisand during her "Color Me Barbra" period, Liza Minnelli in *Cabaret,* Diane Keaton as Annie Hall, Lana Turner in a tight sweater, Barbara Stanwyck looking hard as nails in her *Double Indemnity* wig, a saronged Dorothy Lamour, and — an inside joke, no doubt — Julie Andrews in not-entirely-convincing male disguise from *Victor Victoria.* Any one of them could have fooled a close colleague at first glance, and every one of them was Geoffrey Root. From coiffeur to costuming to cosmetics, he was the Man of a Thousand Faces for the transvestite set.

"That accident scene should be up by now," Padilla said. "Care to look?"

"Would I see anything the experts didn't?"

"Yeah, right. Gnarly stuff. We don't enjoy

this part of the job any more than you do, okay?"

"Okay."

"Some of us have to do this to put chops on the table. We don't get to play at it like some others."

"Okay."

"Everybody wants to play Johnny Jump-Up, Boy Detective. Nobody wants to scrape up someone's guts and carry 'em back to the office in a Hefty bag."

"Okay!" He felt himself turning green.

The lieutenant's glare softened, replaced by a mischievous glint; apparently, a little sadism on the job wasn't frowned upon. He nodded, curled an arm around the monitor, and crooked a finger to mash the tip against one of the photos. He couldn't see it from where he sat, but it was obvious he knew precisely what he was pointing at.

"I'll tell you what convinced me it wasn't coincidence. This" — he thumped the picture — "is how he was got up when he took that header down the ravine. He was on his way to an AIDS benefit, and he was running late, so he was all tarted up for work. I lied about the angora sweater and tight pants, by the way. Bum joke. I should know better: My Uncle Tim asked me to call him Aunt Tina. Root had 'em in a garment bag. They wouldn't fit the opening act. That called for a leotard and tights, and a bowler hat that rolled out from under the dash when the squad-car boys opened the door on the passenger's side."

Valentino leaned forward. It was Root's interpretation of Liza Minnelli, with black hair cropped as she'd worn it in *Cabaret.* That role had established her trademark short-hair look and influenced a generation.

"It's his real hair," Padilla said. "No wig."

"But —"

"Bingo. It's possible — just barely — that one of the big fluffy 'dos he carried from gig to gig came loose, pitched through that hole his head made in the windshield, and just happened to land on the hood, but from where I sit, that's pushing fate with a bull-dozer."

"I agree."

"Whoop-de-doo. I'm not finished. He kept the wigs in hatboxes with the lids clamped tight."

"That narrows the odds."

"You might want to wait till I pause or say 'over' or give you the damn high sign before you dazzle me with your college smarts. There's more."

"Sorry."

"Shut up. The accident investigators said

none of the boxes was empty: Liz and Barbra and Mae and Zsa Zsa and all the rest were accounted for, with their names written on the lids in black Sharpie. All accounted for, that is, because they couldn't know enough to look for the box that *wasn't* there."

"Jayne Mansfield."

"Which means our boy probably took the box with him when he left. Why? He wasn't so shy about covering up his source of inspiration the other two times."

"If you don't have the answer, Lieutenant, I certainly don't."

"So the sleuth is stumped for once." He went on before Valentino could protest. "Also there were no pieces of shattered glass in the loose wig, which confirms the victim wasn't wearing it when he kissed the windshield. So whoever sent Root on his last ride took it out — a dandy two-story job sprayed hard as a carp, like Olivia Newton-Whatserface wore in *Grease* — and plopped it on the hood after the car stopped rolling."

"My God."

Padilla's face was even grimmer than always.

"Not hardly, Boston Blackie. Right now,

111

God's the only One with an alibi we can't bust."

12

Valentino felt sweat pooling at the base of his spine. He got up from the plastic chair and paced the small room, surreptitiously peeling his shirt away from his back, where it had stuck like flypaper. His path described a tight circle: The office was too cluttered with stacks of file folders and yellow legal pads scribbled all over in a cramped hand to encourage any more movement than that. The room was a factory, just as he'd thought, devoted to manufacturing arrests. With great reluctance, the film archivist acknowledged to himself that he and the lieutenant weren't so different after all. What were a corduroy sportcoat with patched elbows and a stiff-as-siding suit between fellow job junkies?

He stopped pacing. "The first two victims were women."

"Also Root wasn't a blonde without the wigwork," Padilla said; "but then neither were half the victims in this creep's book, if we dig down to the roots. Our vic was all the yeller-haired bombshells in Hollywood history, rolled into a lump. Dollars to Ding Dongs he was knocked out or dead before his car went down that ravine. Our boy aimed it at the guardrail, put it in drive, jumped clear, and climbed down afterwards to dress the set. Same basic M.O. as the others."

"You think he was actually riding in the car?"

"Following behind, more likely; less risk of witnesses. Limerick and Ogilvie knew their killer. I went out on a limb there in public, but I'm not nervous. We'll know more when Sacramento processes all the prints in Root's car, or we may not; but he knew our serial nutjob and trusted him enough to tell him where he was headed."

"Are you working this case too?"

"Normally I don't like to butt in. I got plenty on my own plate, to begin with, and the boys who answer to the governor aren't exactly Cub Scouts when it comes to investigating a homicide; but I can't see my way to a tidy bust with all the trimmings if I don't at least ask to ride along. My chief isn't convinced this one's related to the others, so for the time being I'm moonlighting."

"I can't help thinking this character got all his ideas from Beata. When I asked her what she meant by the curse, she mentioned Thelma Todd, Marilyn Monroe, Jean Harlow, Sharon Tate, and Jayne Mansfield. Three of those have already served as crime scenes."

"That checks. There was a trust issue, like I said." He blew a gust of cigarette-flavored air. "Trouble is, by the time we finish questioning all the friends, servants, personal assistants, and presidents of fan clubs, this maniac will have died of old age."

Valentino considered. "You're absolutely right. The same person who killed Beata and Karen killed Root."

"Yeah. Spare me your amateur dick's intuition. Mine's based on experience. The only thing my gut ever told me is when it's time to eat and what I shouldn't have ordered at Pancho O'Hara's Mexican-Irish Pub."

"It's more than that. I just figured out why our killer took away the box labeled Jayne Mansfield."

The officer who'd delivered Valentino to the Beverly Hills station had clocked out, so

115

Padilla drove. He was more comfortable behind the wheel than with his accepted work attire, topped off once again with the suitcoat and necktie.

"Give it to me again," he said.

A by-the-book man, thought his passenger, for all his pose as a department rebel: asking a question that had already been answered in case the answer changed.

"Leaving behind an empty box with Mansfield's name on it would have been too obvious. Too easy. Following the news and waiting for the authorities to connect the dots is part of the fun. It isn't enough just to kill someone and rig the scene to recreate a famous tragedy; he needs to know his work is appreciated. It's like a director reading the trade papers hoping for a rave review and big numbers at the box office."

But that wasn't what had spurred the lieutenant into requesting — no, demanding — his company in the unmarked car. It had happened this way:

Valentino: Did Root live alone?
Padilla: He had a companion, fellow named Sheridan. What their relationship was isn't police business these days.
Valentino: Do we know where he was

116

last night?

Padilla: Troopers are checking his story. But I'm no good at waiting. Let's go.

Valentino: Why me?

Padilla: You speak entertainer. I need an interpreter.

At that hour the streets belonged only to them, late- and early-shifters, and the occasional coyote from the foothills. Fifteen minutes brought them to a retro Spanish/Moroccan hacienda in a neighborhood once crowded with bungalows and motor courts — Nathanael West country — but they'd all given way to bail bondsmen, pawnshops, and quick-check-cash emporia; the dregs of a local economy that never improved. Their facades sported no-nonsense non-decorative grillwork, with forty-watt bulbs burning deep inside to discourage burglars (the kind, Valentino thought acerbically, who wore striped pullovers and little black masks and carried their booty in gunnysacks over one shoulder; anything more sophisticated would have gone through the security systems advertised on their window stickers like a Ginsu knife through gravy).

Eleazar Sheridan, forewarned of their visit by way of Padilla's cell, opened the door of the hacienda, inspected the lieutenant's credentials, and showed them in. He was tall and graying, with a slight stoop, wore a hand-loomed cardigan over a silk polo shirt and pressed khakis, and was obviously composing himself with effort.

"Sorry again for the late hour." Padilla sounded sincere. Valentino (*unfortunately!*) had been in the company of police officials often enough to note the multiple personalities in their possession: suspects (curt), superiors (respectful), upright citizens (cordial), film archivists (barely suppressed rage).

"Not to worry. I don't think I'll be sleeping much for a long time."

The house's interior was refreshingly well-tended, considering the block where it stood. The sunken living room into which the visitors had been led contained a horseshoe-shaped arrangement of eggshell leather sofas and love seats and a round bleached-oak coffee table on a rug with an arabesque border and a teak floor gleaming warmly in the light of low-key lamps with barrel shades. Tasteful African carvings decorated a mantel of very old and weathered cottonwood, above which hung a framed life-size full-body painting of Salome in full harem dress twisting her way through the Dance of the Seven Veils.

Valentino didn't have to step close to identify the model. Geoffrey Root's features, plastic though they were in the original protean sense of the term, were unmistakable despite the exotic makeup and pageboy wig: platinum-blond, as opposed to the usual biblical interpretation of a dusky Mediterranean princess.

There was nothing even slightly masculine about the image. It was anything but preposterous. Anyone unacquainted with the person who'd posed for it would never have suspected it wasn't a woman, and a remarkably attractive woman at that.

Sheridan noted the direction of his guest's gaze. His long features brightened a tint. "That was my present to Jeff, two Christmases ago. I cashed in part of a 401(k) and commissioned the best portrait artist on the Coast. He was so patient about sitting for it. I told him he didn't have to humor me: If he didn't like it, he could stick it in a closet or sell it on eBay. It *is* in questionable taste; but that was my Jeff. You never knew when he was being camp on purpose or just plain clueless. It's one of the things I loved about him. His interests shifted as effortlessly as his personality onstage."

"I'm sorry for your loss," Padilla said; and once again the sympathy seemed genuine.

"I'm investigating what happened as a homicide."

"So you said on the phone." Sheridan's expression changed from grief to curiosity. "Did you say, *'I'm'* investigating? Not *'we're'*?" He looked at the lieutenant's companion, but Valentino was interrupted before he could explain himself.

"He's helping me in an unofficial capacity. The theory I'm testing involves some history he knows a bit about."

As Padilla provided a sketchy account of the theory, their host lowered himself onto one of the sofas, his face slowly turning as pale as the leather. Valentino scarcely noticed, distracted by a pair of shadowy squares he'd spotted on the off-white wall opposite the entrance to the room, one on either side of the fireplace. They appeared to be some kind of mesh, painted to match the background.

"But that's absurd!" Sheridan said, when the narrative ended. "Jeff hadn't an enemy in the world!"

"I get that a lot, sir, and with all respect it's seldom the case. This isn't my first brush with show business. When you're in the limelight, there's always someone you've never met who thinks he knows you. Maybe he's jealous of all the attention you're getting, or maybe he just doesn't like your looks. In this particular case, we have to consider the possibility of a hate crime."

"Because of what we — what Jeff was?" He shook his head, a heartbroken smile on his face. "Both of us have known what we are — were — since we were boys, and children can be crueler than any grown bigot. We'd been called all the names you can think of long before the professional haters spat on us in public and scrawled unspeakable things on our front door. We heard the reports of those other deaths; we suspected they were connected, even if no one else did. If you're saying that some copycat k-killed Jeff because of his lifestyle and tried to make it look like the work of a psycho, I refuse to accept it. I'm in enough pain as it is. What happened to him was a tragedy, not a crime."

"I thought of the copycat angle and rejected it." Now there was no compassion in Padilla's tone, only business. "We're dealing with the original."

"Will you gentlemen please excuse me?" Sheridan got up and hurried out, tugging a handkerchief from a pocket.

Padilla looked uncharacteristically uncomfortable. "Interviewing the widow's the worst part of this job."

Valentino searched his face for irony, found none. The man wasn't a machine after all.

Their host returned. His eyes were red, but his face glistened as if he'd splashed water onto it. "Please forgive me. It's very hard answering all these questions. Why are you so convinced this serial killer is the one?"

"Call it wishful thinking. He's crazy, but he's smart. He worms his way into his victims' confidence, then drops the hammer and arranges the scenario, coldly and methodically. Maybe I'm an optimist, but I don't want to think there are two who operate that way."

"So it isn't a hate crime, then." Sheridan seemed to take comfort from the thought, as if his companion had been swept away by a natural disaster instead of evil intention.

Padilla's face was gloomier than ever. "They all are, in my book."

13

The lieutenant asked Sheridan how well he knew Root's friends. He seemed puzzled by the question.

"As well as he did. Neither of us had any the other didn't. Why?"

"Can you give me their names and numbers? I just want to ask them some questions."

"What sort of questions?"

"The same ones I've been asking you."

Sheridan paled another shade, if that was possible. "Am I a suspect?"

"You were, but I've got a strong hunch you're not as good an actor as your roommate was. I also have to ask you if you or Mr. Root made any new acquaintances recently. A fan, maybe. Someone one or both of you warmed up to right away."

"I can't think of anyone who fits that description, but I'll give you those names and numbers. I don't want our friends harassed," he added, his face darkening.

Padilla's patience was evaporating. Valentino stepped in to make peace. "I'm sorry I never got to see Jeff's act, only the portfolio on his website. Do you have any other pictures we might look at?" He glanced sideways apprehensively, but the lieutenant showed no further annoyance. He seemed to understand that Sheridan needed a neutral few moments to collect himself.

Indeed, the man brightened. "I can do better than that. I can *show* you his act."

He manipulated the arm of the sofa he'd sat in before, opening it to reveal a recess containing a row of switches. He clicked one and the portrait above the fireplace slid up noiselessly into a pocket in the wall, exposing a nylon screen.

Valentino feigned delighted surprise. In fact he'd suspected the room doubled as a home theater: He'd conducted interviews with industry professionals in their private screening rooms and browsed brochures advertising sound equipment throughout his own adventure in theater design; those painted-mesh squares concealed stereo speakers.

A low growl issued from Padilla's throat. His approval had turned to disgust. *Another chunk gone out of my working day watching movies,* his throat seemed to say.

Sheridan didn't notice. He was busy playing eeny, meeny, miny, mo with the switches
in the arm of the sofa. "Jeff preferred film
to DVD and videotape. I came to this town
looking for fame and fortune as an independent moviemaker. So did everyone else; it
didn't pan out, so I got a real job, but when
he found out I knew my way around a
handheld camera he put me to work record-
ing some of his performances. He studied
them over and over, looking for ways to
improve the act. Which one *is* it? Ah!"

There was another click. Suddenly a
rectangular section of the wooden floor
tilted down and rotated 360 degrees, replac-
ing the coffee table and the rug it stood on
with a plain metal cabinet like the kind
room-service waiters used to deliver meals,
bolted to the boards. On the platform, also
securely clamped in place, stood a gray steel
projector, obsolete by today's laser standards, but in what appeared to be excellent
condition.

"He refused to upgrade to digital. See, we
also used it to screen footage of the women
he impersonated, and he was convinced the
only way to study them was in the format
they appeared in originally. Give me a moment while I change reels. Yesterday we saw

125

excerpts from *Some Like It Hot, Red-Headed Woman,* and *The Girl Can't Help It.* You know: Marilyn, Harlow, Jayne, with *Cabaret* as a chaser. At the last minute he'd decided to open with Liza instead of any of the others. The people putting on the benefit were expecting a younger crowd who might not warm to the d-dead stars." As he spoke, he removed the take-up reel from the machine and switched it out with the empty feed reel. Then he fitted another in its place from a flat can he took from inside the cabinet and threaded the end of the film through the pulleys and onto the empty reel. All this was done with a good deal of fumbling, for which he apologized. "I'm handier on the receiving end. The projectionists' union would never issue someone like me a card."

"Harlow?" Padilla whispered to Valentino. "Where'd I hear that name before?"

"Jean Harlow. She's one of the doomed blondes Beata was obsessed with."

"Who killed her, or is that another freaking mystery from the freaking Golden Age of freaking Hollywood?"

"No one, unless you blame her Christian Scientist mother for delaying calling a doctor. She died of kidney failure at age twenty-six."

"Well, I don't see how our scumwad can

rig *that*."

Sheridan dimmed the lights and they made themselves comfortable in the upholstered horseshoe. Valentino couldn't be sure, but he suspected even the hard-boiled Homicide man was impressed with the late Geoffrey Root's performance. Slumped at first on his tailbone in the attitude of supreme resignation, gradually he leaned forward into the light flickering from the screen, his hands gripping his knees and his eyes riveted to the *doppelgangers* of entertainment's most outrageous divas: Buxom Mae West in feathers and a gown shimmering like eelskin, warbling "Frankie and Johnny"; Judy Garland's daughter Liza separating herself from her mother's shadow as she sang, "Put down your knitting, your book and your broom . . ."; platinum-haired Harlow sultrily offering to slip into "something more comfortable" than skintight white silk; Jayne almost falling out of her strapless shift embracing her bleached pet Chihuahuas (comically, they were stuffed toys); and finally the immortal Marilyn "Runnin' Wild," complete with ukulele and trademark wiggle: The film archivist felt his own blood running cold at that point. It had been less than a week since he'd found Beata Limerick gone the same way as that

127

particular candle in the wind.

A ladder-shaped pattern of empty frames streaked across the screen, followed by the flapping of the tag-end of the film and the white glare of a vacant screen.

"Wow!" Valentino said. "She —"

"He." Eleazar Sheridan smiled at him from his perch in the love seat facing him.

"Not bad." Padilla shot to his feet. "Thanks for everything. We'll just take those names and numbers, and let you know if there are any more questions."

But his companion wasn't fooled. The lieutenant had been moved; and he'd definitely been sensitive about the man's loss. The spark of decency was buried as deep as a reel of half-decayed film in an Alaskan landfill; but like the film, Valentino knew it to be there.

They reversed directions, this time along streets waking up to face the day. The sky was turning pewter-colored in the direction of what Kyle Broadhead called "civilization" (meaning the rest of the continental United States) and traffic was picking up. They passed a city street sweeper with its nozzles closed, heading back to the barn at a speed approaching California Normal (meaning ten miles above the urban limit).

Ray Padilla drove with his eyes bolted to the road, the long muscle in his jaw standing out like braided steel cable. "Next to pumping the grieving next of kin for information, I hate this part the worst. You can't sweat the truth out of 'em without probable cause, and death has a way of washing the vic in the blood of the lamb. Any flaws in his character never existed. Everyone who ever died unexpectedly turns into a saint."

Valentino muttered something he hoped was appropriate. He was only half-listening.

"You were a big help in there," his companion went on. "I brought you along to give me the benefit of your showbiz know-how, not wangle a free show."

"I was stalling for time to think."

"As for instance."

"I wish I knew. It's like when we were at Beata's, and again when you told me how you found Karen Ogilvie. The connections to Monroe and Todd were obvious, but I didn't see them until something jogged my memory."

"You were quick enough to spot the Mansfield thing."

"By then I was looking for it, or something like it. This is different. There's a common theme apart from the similarities to the deaths of movie stars, I'm sure of it — I felt

129

as if I were just inches away when that film was running — but I couldn't quite jump the gap. It's like needing to yawn and not being able to. You can't force it. It has to come on its own."

Padilla yawned; whether he was mocking Valentino or truly exhausted was impossible to tell. Probably it was a little of both, but when the other spoke again he seemed to understand.

"It's more like an itch you can't reach. You can throw your back out trying to get to it. So you try to think of something else until it lets up."

"Is that what you do? Stop thinking about it?"

"Yeah, but don't tell anybody I said so. My chief's got the idea the city isn't paying me *not* to think about my work. Acts like it's coming out of his pocket."

"It is. Part of it, anyway."

"I'll give him his part back while I get some shut-eye."

He dropped his passenger off in front of The Oracle. The sun was visible now, a bloodshot orb that reminded Valentino of the grit in his eyelids. He decided there was something to that Sandman story parents told their children: The grains scratched his corneas when he blinked.

130

The extension ladder belonging to Peter, the electrician, leaned against the marquee in its bag, an oversize version of the ones the city put on parking meters when they were out of service. The ladder reminded him of a strip of blank film, a line of empty squares that at the start of a feature promised everything, but at the end offered nothing but the signal that it was time to leave the theater. The image stayed with him as he dragged himself up the steep stairs to his apartment in the projection booth, and was the last thing he thought of after he threw himself onto the rollaway bed without bothering to take off even his shoes and drifted away from a landscape that seemed to be nothing more than a montage of death scenes spliced together for a documentary about Hidden Hollywood.

As he slept, Beata Limerick, Karen Ogilvie, and Geoffrey Root leaned over him and shouted the answer; but when he awoke with a shock, it was garbled by three voices crying simultaneously, drowning one another out. He spent what remained of the morning trying to recall what they'd said, but then he took Padilla's advice and stopped trying.

14

Kyle Broadhead was the only man Valentino had ever known who owned his own tuxedo. Full ownership of elegant evening address seemed to have passed out of fashion with the death of Dean Martin.

As the Film Preservation Department's designated fund-raiser ("arm-twister, confidence man, gigolo, professional blackmailer," were his preferred terms), he wore it frequently to black-tie parties: "I never eat or drink at these functions, Val. They're the equivalent of an open guitar case on the corner of Sunset and Vine and a rudimentary knowledge of 'Stairway to Heaven.' If I look like I'm enjoying myself, I'll come away empty-handed."

The garment, out of date as it was, double-breasted with a shawl collar as wide as a six-lane highway, was an uncommonly fine one of heavy silk and satin, but it had almost as many miles on it as the man who wore it.

While trying it on in preparation for his nuptials, the professor had put his hand through the elbow of the dinner jacket, signaling the need for a new fitting. "They just don't make them like they used to," he grumbled.

"They don't make them at all anymore," his friend informed him. "Is that a watch pocket?"

"If cell phones get any smaller, it'll be right back in style."

It behove his best man to accompany him to his tailor of choice, whose probable extinction the groom stubbornly refused to accept. But as was usual with that infuriating man, the towering odds in favor of obsolescence in the ever-changing geography of Los Angeles were suspended. After Valentino had burned a quarter tank of gas looking in all the places the shop should have been but wasn't, they pulled up at last in front of a squat ancient building with a faded striped awning surrounded by looming skyscrapers. A curling cardboard sign in the window had read FREE ALTERATIONS before someone had crossed out the first word and scribbled REASONABLY PRICED above it.

When they opened the glass-paneled door, a copper bell mounted on a spring clip tinkled and a pleasant masculine odor of leather and crisp fabric puffed out. Walls of yellow plaster wore framed blow-up photographs of Tom Mix, a positively adolescent Cary Grant, Emil Jannings, and other close contemporaries; former satisfied customers, Valentino supposed, wondering how the place had managed to stay afloat so long after they'd taken their business to the Great Beyond.

A door behind an oak-framed glass counter admitted a middle-aged Korean in white lawn shirtsleeves and pinstripe trousers with a yellow tape measure draped around his neck. "May I help you gentlemen?"

"Where's Irving?" Broadhead asked.

"I'm afraid he retired fifteen years ago."

"I get a card signed by him every Christmas."

"That was Mr. Feingold's wish, expressed on the occasion of his ninety-ninth birthday, the day he retired."

"Where can I reach him?"

The young man blinked.

Broadhead turned to Valentino. "Irving made all the bespoke prison uniforms for George Raft."

"I always thought that was an urban legend."

"You didn't know Raft. Cinematically

speaking, he spent more time in stir than the Birdman of Alcatraz, and he hated the thought of looking frumpy."

"Perhaps I can be of assistance," the Korean said. "I apprenticed under Mr. Feingold."

"I'd feel better about it if you had cigarette burns on your vest and a Yiddish accent."

"I don't smoke, but —" He cleared his throat and released a string of guttural sounds from which the words *"alter kocker"* stood out. Valentino burst into laughter.

"What was so funny?" demanded Broadhead, when he paused for breath.

"Nothing," he said, wiping tears from his eyes. "Unless you ushered one summer when Sid Rugmann managed the Rialto Theater in Fox Forage, Indiana."

The tailor snapped his tape measure taut with the crack of a whip, raising his eyebrows in anticipation. There was no trace of humor on his face.

It turned positively grim when Broadhead unzipped the garment bag he'd carried in and showed him the huge rip in the elbow of the jacket. "I'd have to re-weave it, sir. A new one won't cost you much more."

"I'm getting ready for a wedding, not supersizing a soda."

"Very well. I estimate six months."

"I'm getting married in three. What's the holdup?"

"This fabric has to be ordered from Italy. The dockworkers have been on strike since December. Even if they settle the dispute tomorrow, I can't make any promises beyond what I said."

The professor's eyes narrowed. "You *did* learn from Irving. You ought to fly the Jolly Roger out front."

Later, seated in the fitting room in his shirtsleeves and boxers awaiting the return of the Korean, Broadhead hummed along with an easy-listening station piped in through speakers. Valentino averted his gaze from the scars on the man's bare legs; fresh evidence of his long-ago incarceration in a Yugoslavian prison, charged with espionage.

"I won't ask again what the joke was," he said. "But I was afraid you'd become hysterical."

Valentino nodded. "I was, kind of. It was the first thing that struck me funny in days."

"One of the advantages of age is you grow accustomed to losing your friends. It's also one of the disadvantages. In the end you cease to care about anyone's mortality, least of all your own. You don't buy into that curse nonsense, do you?"

"Beata did, and she was nobody's fool.

You have to admit a lot of top-billed blondes didn't live long enough to check into the Motion Picture Home."

"I could name as many or more top-billed brunettes who didn't either, but no one would listen. Peroxide is a powerful aphrodisiac. Anyway, there's more to this funk you're in than silly superstition, or how close you were to Beata. You hardly knew Karen Ogilvie."

"I didn't know the latest victim at all."

He told Broadhead about Geoffrey Root, not leaving out Eleazar Sheridan's moving show of grief, which had affected the film archivist more than he might have expected. His mentor, steeped even deeper in the history of the motion-picture community than his protégé, picked up on the similarities to the Mansfield case immediately, and agreed with Padilla's theory that their serial killer was involved; also with Valentino's regarding the murderer's motive in carrying away the box that had contained the wig he'd left at the scene.

"He's a frustrated puppet master, for sure," he said. "How does Padilla think he did it?"

"If he was riding in the car, he made some excuse to pull over. He's partial to blunt instruments, so the lieutenant's expecting the medical examiner to find evidence of concussion or worse. Then he drove the car the rest of the way to the top of the ravine, got out, and pushed it over by hand. Sheridan said he thought Root was alone, so our killer might have been following him and took advantage of a red light or a stop sign at some lonely crossroads — the area was full of those — jerked open the driver's side door, and struck him that way. You know the rest."

"Everything but why."

"Padilla said that's the prosecutor's problem. *His* job is to nail the guy while there's a blonde left in Southern California. His words," Valentino added.

"I like a man who knows his duty. If he's as good a detective as he sounds, he's working on a way to be ahead of the killer for once."

Valentino smiled grimly. "I don't think Ray Padilla believes in crystal balls."

"He doesn't need one. He has you. Who was the other blonde Beata mentioned after Marilyn, Thelma, and Jayne?"

His friend felt his face grow pale again.

The tailor returned, carrying a bolt of black fabric; but by then his customer was stepping back into his trousers, with Valentino waiting impatiently for him to finish.

"It's only a guess, remember. In any case, how can we act without knowing who he is or the name of his next victim?"

Valentino was driving; if not exactly aimlessly, in the general direction of the UCLA campus, where both men did their best thinking. "It would be a gathering of some kind, not just one person. So far he's staged every murder as close to the original as possible. There's no reason to believe he'd deviate from the plan."

"You mean apart from the fact he's crazy?"

"Insane people can be even more conscientious about following a pattern than rational ones. Who do we know who's planning a party?"

"That should be easy; L.A. not being much of a party town."

"Kyle, can you for once put aside your natural inclination to sneer at everything?"

"I'll try; but you have to understand it's how I cope. If it weren't for a well-developed defense mechanism, I wouldn't be sitting here, watching you shatter every traffic law in California."

"I'm sorry." He stopped with a chirp at a

light that had just turned red. A Range Rover the size of Grauman's Chinese Theater shot through the intersection, blasting its horn for a block.

"Think about it," Broadhead said. "Every weekend — and some don't wait that long — someone's celebrating an award or a nomination or a movie wrap or a plum part or a retirement, and that's just the industry. This is the largest city in the western world and one of the most gregarious. On any given evening it makes *The Great Gatsby* look like *Castaway.* And we don't even know this guy's thinking what we're thinking."

"Still, it beats no theory at all. Let's go over it again. In each case, the murder was committed by someone the victim trusted."

"It's a wonder they lived as long as — never mind. On the day she was killed, Beata Limerick wasn't expecting anyone but you. You never killed anyone; I'm not *that* cynical. Marilyn Monroe. Karen Ogilvie spent the night with friends, but as far as we know she was alone when the murderer came. No sign of a break-in, so she must have let him in. Thelma Todd. Geoffrey Root — the only male victim, but his dress and behavior put him just inside the perpetrator's M.O. — was on his way to a paying gig when he was ambushed. Jayne Mansfield. This is shaping up like one of those cheesy shock-sexploitation flicks they used to show in drive-in theaters. Green."

Belatedly, Valentino saw the light had changed. He started forward, not before the driver behind beeped twice, almost politely.

"I know what you mean. Harriet says when The Oracle is up and running, I can recoup my investment in three years if I cater to that trade; but I can't even bring myself to screen that kind of trash, much less —"

He slammed on the brakes. Broadhead seized the dashboard in both hands. "Are you *trying* to duplicate the scene of the last murder?"

The same cordial driver who'd tooted at him earlier leaned on his horn button. Valentino held up an apologetic hand and resumed driving.

"Forgive me, Kyle. Since I'm pushing my luck at the wheel already, do me a favor: Look up Lieutenant Padilla's number and give him a ring." He handed the professor his phone.

"If you want to turn yourself in for being a menace on the road, you should call Traffic Enforcement instead."

"Sheridan."

"Root's partner? What makes you think he — ?"

"No, I'm convinced he's innocent. But he said something that showed me how dense we've — I've been."

"So you're going to keep me in the dark until I goggle at you along with all the rest during the Big Reveal? I should tell you, Nigel Bruce ruined Dr. Watson for me."

"Maybe Basil Rathbone didn't want to look like a fool if he turned out to be wrong. I probably am, but if I'm not, I think I just figured out who killed them all and how he got in."

15

"It's ringing." Broadhead grinned and winked. "I always wanted to do this."

"Kyle, don't —"

"Shhh! Lieutenant Padilla, please. Tell him Valentino is calling about the Marilyn murders. Yes, I'll hold." He hummed, cupped his hand over the mouthpiece. "ABBA. I'm disappointed."

"What did you expect, the theme from *Dragnet*?"

"Anything but 'Honey, Honey.'" He took away his hand. "Lieutenant Padilla? Please hold for Valentino." Chuckling, he thrust the phone at the driver.

"What the hell!" was the first thing Valentino heard.

He glared at Broadhead, who appeared to be enjoying the scenery. They were passing along a bleak section of Sunset, all parking lots and major-appliance boxes rigged out for habitation. "I apologize for my friend,

Lieutenant. I thought of a lead you might —"

"Save your sorries for yourself, buster. Tell me what you're doing meddling in an open homicide investigation."

Buster? "I wasn't. I just thought of something Eleazar Sheridan said when you and I visited him."

"Glad you remember I was there. Not that I give a rat's tuckus what an amateur thinks he heard that I didn't. I ask questions, I listen to the answers, I bring 'em back to the office and turn 'em over till they're done on both sides, and if I don't like the way they turn out I go back and ask the same questions and nine times or ten I get a whole different batch of answers. In the real world, pal, we don't gather all the suspects in a ritzy dining room and spill everything we know. We don't get confessions that way. What we get is the big clam."

Pal? He pulled over to the curb. Negotiating L.A. traffic was challenge enough without digesting a lecture on police procedure at the same time.

Broadhead, staring at him now, mouthed, "What?"

He shook his head. "Hold on, Lieutenant. No matter what you said last time we spoke, I know I'm still on your books because I knew two of the victims. It's only natural I'd want to look into the case."

"Nuts. You take in an all-night Charlie Chan film festival and you think you're Number One Son. You don't hang around after the credits finish rolling to see the cops try to assemble the mess of pieces he scraped up into a picture they can sell the prosecutor. Even when that makes it to the screen, the editors or whatever they're called snip out ninety-nine percent of the grunt-work involved, because nobody'd sit through a movie that's three months long. We do, because we're paid to."

"That's why I called, to help save you some of that time. I think I can identify the murderer."

"Me, too; which is why I put Sheridan in custody."

A truck rumbled past, shaking pieces out of the cracked pavement. Valentino stuck a finger in the ear on that side. "I told Broadhead just a minute ago I think Sheridan's innocent."

"Based on what? And what are you yelling about?"

He lowered his voice. The truck was a block away. "That's why I called you. I —"

"You had somebody call for you and dick around. But, hey, if you say Sheridan's clean, that settles it. I'll get the D.A. on the horn right away and tell him my pet college egghead spoke up for our most valuable perp."

"You think he killed his partner?"

"Not just Root. The whole shebang, Limerick and Ogilvie too."

"But why?"

"That's our job, and it's half-done. The job says I take in everything, even crackpot theories by amateurs who spend too much time at the cineplex. 'Come on down,' like they say on *The Price Is Right*. It's my dinner party, but I won't hog it. I'll hang on every harebrained word you have to say, sucking piping-hot joe from the machine down the hall in a mug my kid made for me in summer camp."

Through Padilla's glass wall, Valentino watched Eleazar Sheridan, his face gray and blank, being conducted down the hall by a plainclothesman whose own face looked as if it had been left to soak too long, hanging in loose folds pegged in place with eyes as flat as thumbtacks. The suspect's wrists were shackled behind his back.

The lieutenant's desk was piled high as before. He pulled out the bottom drawer, rested his feet on it with the ankles crossed,

146

and blew steam from his mug. He hadn't lied about that. It was ceramic, somewhat lopsided, and the handle canted off at an inconvenient angle. He ignored it, raising the receptacle by wrapping his hand around it, like a cup of saki in Benihana's. His initials were scooped into the side; Valentino thought at first it read R.I.P.

"How's that water?" he asked Broadhead. "We're fresh out of Perrier. Sorry as hell. Hoping to buy one of those fancy water stations like in Safeway soon as we find a customer for the department armored half-track. Since the President stopped us from buying surplus equipment from the army, chief says holding onto it's a PR issue."

The professor drank from his Ozarka bottle. "It's refreshing, thank you. I like your office. Who did it for you, Eliot Ness?"

He got a blank stare back. They were two of a kind, Valentino noted: Men with edgy senses of humor who failed to acknowledge it in others. Their host snatched up his handset and hit a button. "Can I get an ETA on that interview room? Seriously?" He banged the receiver into the cradle. "Gang boys broke up a brawl this morning in East L.A.: 'with chains and knives,' like they used to say on *Adam-12.* They're re-running it on broadband every night this week. Now, *there* was a cop show. That pair of squaddies got more action in one tour than all Downtown gets in a year." He slurped coffee, sighed. "If one of our vics was Julia Roberts, maybe a little old homicide case would get first crack."

"Let's hope for the best."

"Kyle." Valentino spoke wearily. He was the only man in the room on his feet; not that there was another chair available, but if there had been one he'd have declined it.

"Well, we'll get our turn. What we got won't expire while the Jets and the Sharks are singing for Officer Krupke." Padilla showed his lower teeth in his *Werewolf of London* grin. "Yeah, I tune in to AMC now and again. You were there, son. You heard everything I heard; according to you, you heard more, but we'll come to that. It's what we underpaid public servants *don't* hear sets us scrambling for our Miranda cards. He made out like he didn't know Beata Limerick or Karen Ogilvie from the Olsen twins. What he didn't say was how he met Root: waiting tables at a political fund-raiser for a man running for Governor of California on a gay rights platform, where Root was performing. He was Peggy Lee that night, our informant says. His 'Why Don't You Do Right' brought down the house."

"What's incriminating about that?"

"You ain't seen nothing yet. Who said that?"

"Al Jolson," Valentino and Broadhead said simultaneously.

"Rhetorical question," growled Padilla. "Our informant was headwaiter that night. We found him through the same catering firm Sheridan told us he worked for before he retired — on his partner's salary. You need to remember that. This headwaiter's working in Beverly Hills now, pulling down a couple of hundred thou a year, not counting tips, showing the guests to their tables in the Wilshire dining room. That's how good he is, and why he can tell you years later who waited on which table and where. Sheridan was in charge of three stations that night. How he met Root, Root was invited to join one of those parties after the show. It was Karen Ogilvie did the inviting.

"It was her party," he added. "Well, you being a 'film detective,' maybe you can figure out who was sitting at one of the other tables Sheridan waited on." He looked from one silent face to the other. "What, no duet this time? Sure, it was the Limerick woman. She had the rack of lamb: well-done, says the headwaiter, who disapproved. I guess Ogilvie didn't offend him with her

149

order, because he couldn't recall what she ate, only that she was there and had all her other guests move one chair down so Root could sit next to her."

Valentino said, "Waiting on someone doesn't make you an acquaintance."

"It did where Geoffrey Root was concerned. Now, even our headwaiter wasn't aware who Limerick and Ogilvie were, and he's better at remembering dishes and stations than names. But we showed him the victims' photos, and the rest came pouring out."

Broadhead said, "I can think of a line of questioning that would destroy your case in court, Lieutenant; and as the head of my department I deal with real lawyers in the real world."

"It wouldn't take Perry Mason to rip up what I told you. But Sheridan lived off Root, and when one person exists on another person's money, you can smell the motive way ahead of a plate of burned lamb chops. Once we get Sheridan into that interview room, *my* money's on a lovers' tiff and a threat to cancel his meal ticket. That's rage. If we get a break and there was a will or some kind of agreement like that in place — one Root never got the chance to change — that's greed, and I'd trade all

150

the rest of the sins for just those two."

Valentino had seen the joy of anticipation on a man's face only in his mirror before he screened a forgotten classic film for the first time. He should have been appalled, but it made him feel a millimeter closer to the detective lieutenant, who was human in at least one area.

He shook his head. "That might convict Sheridan for Root's murder, but he had no reason to kill the others."

"He did if he wanted us to think just the way we have been, that they were all done by a serial killer with a grudge against bombshell blondes. We might've gone on for years, talking to shrinks and psychics and scouring the country for Hannibal the Cannibal, when we should've been looking for a garden-variety cold-blooded sponge with an eye for the main chance. Meanwhile, he might just have racked up a couple more Hollywood-themed murders just to make sure we were paying attention."

He set down his cup, making sure it didn't tip over on its uneven base. "It ain't as poetic, boys; in my book, it's more evil still. A homicidal maniac can no more stop himself than an earthquake or a hurricane. One of 'em can kill a hundred innocents and I'd be the first to applaud when some bleeding-heart judge sentences him to therapy, but anybody who'd snuff out two lives just so he can tuck the one he wanted to take in between 'em needs to be cut up and fed to a goat."

"I can't say I disagree," Valentino said, "although I'm not so sure about the goat. But you were there, Lieutenant. Even you were moved by his emotional state."

"Remember that next time you string together some old meller about sourpuss flatfeet with rock heads and stone hearts. He could've faked it. There are certain types that can throw a lie detector for a loop. More likely it was genuine. If you can work up enough of a mad to kill someone, you can squeeze out real tears. Most of them, the ones that aren't actual psychopaths, feel sorry for what they did, even miss the person as hard as if he fell off a cliff or got run over by the wieniemobile. I always get nervous whenever some Raskolnikov I nabbed gets on the stand to testify in his defense; they've been known to sway juries away from ironclad evidence. But that's the DA's headache, and if it goes the other way and they seal him up in Q for ninety-nine years and a day, I won't feel a bit more sorry than if he flipped the victim's survivors the bird in open court.

"That's my job, boys. It don't pay a couple of hundred thou and tips, but I'd rather deliver a solid case than overdone mutton any day."

His telephone rang. Interview Room C was ready.

16

Sometimes, the movies got it right.

And sometimes, the people in charge of such things cast against type.

For all he revered the fantasy world of motion pictures, Valentino had always thought certain things were purely the invention of screenwriters. That a real-life police department in the twenty-first century should play the good-cop-bad-cop card, straight off the back lot, came as much of a surprise as who was cast in those roles.

Watching, with Kyle Broadhead, through the one-way glass into Interview Room C, the film archivist saw the plainclothesman with the face that had been soaked too long and pinned up with thumbtacks had been chosen to play the heavy. He inhabited the role to the full, pumping himself up puffer-fish fashion to what seemed twice his size for the benefit of the stricken man seated with his now-unfettered hands making wet patches on the fake wood-printed veneer of the table in the center of the cramped chamber. The transformation from weary civil servant to authoritarian brute was complete, and took place before the eyes of the Film Preservation crew.

Padilla, by contrast, sat opposite the suspect with his hands folded almost prayer-like on the table, his face arranged into a mask of sympathy. (Tellingly, his palms left no marks at all.) From time to time he murmured something in soothing tones so low the microphone failed to pick them up.

"The frauds," murmured Broadhead. "You wonder anyone still falls for it."

"We're watching from the cheap seats, don't forget. I imagine it's different sitting stage front."

"What makes you an expert?"

"I'm not sure. Maybe I've been too much among cops of late."

"And too little among people. Let's just go."

"Beata would never forgive me if I didn't see the thing through."

"Beata's dead."

"That's just it. If she were alive, she'd probably tell me to let go. Dead, she's harder to get along with."

"So you've given up on your hunch?"

"I don't know. It all seemed so simple until I entered this building. What was it General Norman Schwarzkopf said about battle plans?"

"They never survive the first engagement with the enemy."

"We're not exactly among enemies. But like I said, they do this all the time. Anything you and I or anyone else could come up with they've already considered and set aside."

A circular speaker like the ones installed in the drive-through lanes of fast-food restaurants allowed them to hear what was taking place inside. A number of interested parties, some in uniform, others in suits and sportcoats, had gathered to eavesdrop. In some office much quieter and more private than Padilla's glass cubicle, authorities with clout would be listening to the same conversation in leather-upholstered comfort.

Cuttle: Go over it again, let's. You two got your little panties in a wad. Root told you to pack up your crap and skedaddle, gave you a deadline, which was his big mistake, because it gave you time to cook up your little game of dominoes: Beata Limerick. Click!

Karen Ogilvie. Click! Geoffrey Root. Click.

Sheridan: I didn't. He didn't! It was never that way between Jeffy and me.

Cuttle: You're a goddamn liar! I can stomach a killer, even a yellow dress-it-up one that'd clock a couple of old ladies to cover up his mess, but I can't abide a sneaky mealy-mouthed goddamn liar!

Even Broadhead, cynic that he was, flinched when the sergeant bellowed in Sheridan's face, close enough to flick it with spittle.

Padilla unfolded his hands and grasped Cuttle's wrist.

Padilla: Back off, Sergeant. Everybody lies sometime, especially when he's afraid. Eleazar — can I call you that? I can't think of a nickname —

Sheridan: Sherry's okay. That's what Jeffy called me.

Padilla: Sherry, there's nothing to be afraid of here. What you did, it was desperation behind it. People think you had a cushy position, being looked after, all the comforts somebody with money can buy; but it comes with a price. There isn't a juror in the world who wouldn't understand what it means to depend on somebody who uses that dependence like a whip to keep you down.

Cuttle: Enough of that shrink talk. I'm crying big fat snotty tears — for that poor pink powder-puff you threw through his windshield, ripping his face —

Padilla: Lay off that.

Valentino saw a crack in the masquerade. The lieutenant really seemed to think his partner was going too far.

But then, some of the best actors in Hollywood worked for the Los Angeles Police Department.

There was a long hiatus while Eleazar Sheridan sat slumped with his shoulders shaking, water streaming down his cheeks in glistening rivulets and forming a puddle around the wet marks his palms had made on the table. Cuttle (hamming it up, Valentino thought) paced the room in rapid steps, like a big cat left in his cage long past feeding, Padilla (a paean to subtlety) sitting back watching the pathetic creature across from him with the patience of — well, not quite a saint, but the director of any religious epic would have been satisfied to include him in the production.

The rest was more of the same, as the detectives confronted the suspect, one accusing, the other compassionate, with the discrepancy in his earlier statements, chiefly the fact that Beata Limerick and Karen Ogilvie were no strangers to him, and using the headwaiter's statement as a club (identifying him only as an ominous "eyewitness"), slugging away at his denials until he fell into a paroxysm of hysterical uncertainty.

Padilla's right, Valentino thought. *The real world bears no resemblance to entertainment.*

"I don't remember any of them." This came from the depths of exhaustion; of a body whose glands had wrung themselves dry of tears.

"You saying our witness is a goddamn liar, you goddamn liar?" Cuttle never let up. Valentino wondered if he stayed in character all day long, and what his home life must be like.

"No! I don't remember anything about that evening except meeting Jeffy. He was the most — why would I want to kill him?"

"We been over that. We got it all on tape, with Dolby. You want us to play it back, or would you rather wait for the transcript, read it over a soothing cup of Darjeeling,

159

you miserable piece of —"

"Take a break, Sergeant."

From the look on Cuttle's unmade face, this was a departure from the script. The man's relentless performance seemed to have had a greater negative effect on his partner than on its intended target. He was a veteran, however, and didn't tip his hand, storming out and banging the door shut behind him. Outside, his pace slowed to that of a man unsure of where he was heading. He passed the two civilians without a glance, deflating a little with each step until by the time he'd reached the end of the hall the Hulk had returned to normal size. The LAPD came with its own brand of CGI.

Inside the interview room, Padilla, with the weary patience of a man whose sympathies had worn nearly through, told it all again to Sheridan, as matter-of-factly as if he'd been present when the two men had had the quarrel he was certain had taken place.

"He never said a harsh word to me in my life, nor I to him."

The lieutenant heaved a sigh. It seemed so authentic, Valentino stored away the information against the day (please, Lord, no) he found himself on the other end of it. "I didn't want to bring this up, Sherry.

Things would have gone easier on you if you came through with it on your own. You were overheard fighting about money. We talked to your neighbors. He wasn't sure of the date, but it was more than a week ago, not long before these killings started."

The man in custody went on staring at the table, making no more sounds than a grown man struggling not to sob out loud.

"We're not monsters." Padilla's tone was so low the listeners outside had to lean close to the speaker to hear. "We've seen it before, and we understand up to a point. An older man living off a younger instead of the other way around; well, that's humiliating. After a while he begins to resent what seemed like generosity in the beginning. I'm not saying Jeffy lorded it over you. I try not to speak ill of the dead. But people are human, and things get said in the heat of anger that can't be taken back afterwards. We understand, we do. Up to a point."

He was expressing the same sentiments as before, with slightly different words; but then Cuttle had done the same with his unrelenting attack on Sheridan's humanity.

Still no response. The lieutenant seemed to have expected none; certainly he didn't appear to be annoyed. He pushed himself to his feet.

161

"I'll give you some time to yourself. You can still turn this around. You're not the first person that got tossed out on his ear. You're sure not the first that panicked and did what he thought he had to do to avoid it. Any jury would see it your way with the right defense; and if you pitch in and help us put this one to rest."

Valentino was so mesmerized by the pathetic figure hunched over the table — so different from the gracious, grieving man he'd visited in the comfortable home he'd shared with his life's partner — he wasn't aware the lieutenant had joined him, Broadhead, and the curious policemen gathered before the window until he heard the familiar terrier's yelp.

"I'm surprised we didn't crack this one the first day with so many men working the case. Don't any of you have a piece of scum of your own to lock up?"

The crowd dispersed, leaving the two visitors alone with the real Ray Padilla.

17

Broadhead, jaded though he was, said, "Huh!" He, too, had been taken in by the lieutenant's charade.

Valentino shook his head. "It's possible he killed Root out of desperation, but I can't believe he'd commit two cold-blooded murders just to cover his tracks."

"That's what he's counting on," Padilla said. "These sensitive types can be the toughest to crack. Give me one of these gangbangers anytime; they come swaggering into the interview hard as a day-old KFC biscuit and come out twenty minutes later bawling for their mommies. But we'll get him. Give him a spell in there alone and he'll gush forth like Old Faithful."

"Who's this neighbor you claim heard them fighting over money?"

The lieutenant looked uncomfortable, rare event. He lowered his voice.

"It'll be public record soon enough, but if

you spill this before we get his signature on a confession I'll put you in the cell next to his. We got it from a can-and-bottle collector combing through a city trash can on the corner by the house. He came in to file a complaint against space aliens stealing from his stash and the rest just sort of spilled out."

Broadhead said, "And you're going to take that into open court?"

"If Sheridan cooperates, it won't be necessary. I've dealt with this type enough times to know when they're on the level. Sometimes we can keep the rest out of the transcript, but if a half-smart P.D. sees through the Sears suit we'll give him and his first bath and shave since last fall, it'll be like Christmas morning for the defense. Which is why we can't let our suspect find out till he incriminates himself."

"You believe the story?" Valentino asked.

"I do. Some of us work at this job. And you didn't hear Sheridan deny it once we dropped it in his lap. Now, what's this important piece of information you're sitting on that'll blow this case wide open?"

Broadhead spoke before Valentino could open his mouth. "You say that like you're interested; but I can't help feeling you're being ironic."

164

"Kyle."

Padilla said nothing, waiting for an answer to his question.

"It was something Sheridan said."

"You mean just now? Gee, I thought I was paying attention."

"I mean when we were talking with him in his house. He said he was inept at operating a projector."

"Shucks, I can barely work a DVD player. That wouldn't clear me if I had his motive and no alibi for last night. If he's got one for any of the others, it'll push over when I breathe on it."

"It didn't register at first. Then I remembered that Beata insisted on following the rules of the projectionists' union. The day she died, she was going to treat me to a screening of her print of *The Sandpipers.*"

"You should take a day off. Even I put away the rubber hose once every couple of weeks to grill burgers in the backyard."

"What I'd like to know is what happened to the professional projectionist she had lined up for the demonstration."

Padilla's face showed nothing, but he jerked his head in the direction of his office.

When they were inside with the door closed he said, "Keep it low. If I make captain over this deal, maybe they'll give me walls that go all the way to the ceiling."

"Two of the victims, Root included, had projectors set up: Beata for the reason I gave you, Root so he could study the celebrities he imitated and evaluate his own performances. If he used the same service Beata did, and we can find out if Karen Ogilvie used it around the time she was killed —"

The lieutenant dragged over the closest file folder and scribbled something on it. "We'll look into it."

"Seriously? You're not just blowing me off?"

"See, that's what I mean about mixing up movie cops with the real thing. We don't stop investigating when we got a prime candidate for arrest. If I'd got into that habit, taking a chance on my case blowing up in my face in a courtroom because I overlooked an important detail, I'd still be riding around Watts in a blue-and-white."

In the passenger seat riding away from headquarters, Broadhead was thoughtful.

"I'm beginning to think I should make that donation to the widows-and-orphans fund. A man like that could change all my opinions about cops."

"You think Sheridan did it too?"

"Let's just say I've been around longer than you and seen the elephant, and he doesn't always turn out to be Dumbo. If Padilla's right about that bum —"

"Homeless person."

"It's just us, Val. I've got tenure. I don't have to be politically correct. As I was saying: If Padilla's right about that unfortunate victim of our cold harsh society, Sheridan had a made-to-order reason to set up his partner."

"I agree; but I don't see him for the others."

"Who's to say that once you decide to break the most important law of God and man the life of anyone else matters? It makes more sense than your phantom projectionist."

"We're drifting away pretty quickly from the original scenario, that our killer's got some insane resentment toward everyone who fits Beata's curse theory."

"Not quickly enough for me. *The Silence of the Lambs* is a great flick, but it wouldn't be the first time a successful idea opened the floodgates to every schlockmeister in the industry. I grew up on Nero Wolfe and Ellery Queen. Their creators put in a lot of overtime creating plausible motivations for their perpetrators. Whipping up a sensational murder on no other premise than the murderer had a bad experience in potty

167

training is just plain lazy."

"Now you're even beginning to sound like Padilla."

"Why not? We could use him on the debate team. He works on pure reason."

"Why are you trying so hard to sell me on Sheridan?"

"Because I love you. You have a gift. Where others see a plain rock you see the gem under the dirt. Padilla's got the same gift, only in reverse: He turns over rocks to expose the slime underneath to sun and air. You both serve mankind, but I'd rather hang out with you. Stop trying to do his job and concentrate on yours."

Valentino was touched by his friend's concern; he rarely cracked his hard-boiled façade. "Can it be you're mellowing in the glow of matrimonial bliss?"

"Let's just say I'm enjoying my second childhood. At age twelve I was too busy studying for my master's to appreciate the first."

They drove a few blocks in silence. Then Broadhead said, "You didn't share your other theory with Padilla. About the gathering."

"It was a long shot, to begin with. After what he said about Sheridan it just seemed silly."

"You're probably right."

But, Valentino thought, *it had probably seemed just as silly the first time.*

They entered the parking lot adjacent to the old power station now occupied by the Film Preservation Department. Something chimed. Valentino pulled into a slot and glanced at the dashboard clock. Ten minutes past the hour. It couldn't be the bell tower marking the time.

The chime was repeated. "What the devil is that?"

Broadhead said, "I think you've got a text."

"I never get a text. I don't even know how to text."

"And they call *me* a dinosaur." He snatched Valentino's cell from the console between them, glanced at the screen, and handed it over without a word.

Sure enough, there was a message. He turned off the phone.

"It's from my electrician."

"Do you want me to answer him for you?"

"I can do that in person. Would you like to see what The Oracle marquee looks like when it's lit up?"

"I've been counting the years." The professor looked at the building, a bleak obelisk

169

whose construction appeared to have pre-dated the invention of windows. "Anything to avoid another intimate moment with Ruth. Should we invite Harriet?"

Valentino punched the POWER button and brought up speed dial. The phone rang twice and Harriet's voice came on.

"How's it going, Hawkshaw? Close the case yet?"

"Padilla did. In my face." He told her about the marquee.

"This isn't going to be a replay of last time, is it?"

"Are you interested or not?" He'd had his fill of pessimism for that week.

"Give me a minute to change, then come pick me up."

"We're not dressing."

"I wasn't thinking of shaking out the old ball gown. I doubt you want me showing up for the Big Event in a smock smeared all over with gray-matter."

Broadhead borrowed the phone to call Fanta. She said she was up to her elbows in case law history, but wouldn't mind putting aside *Warner Brothers versus Olivia de Havilland* to watch someone flip an electric switch. He hit END and returned the instrument. "Mind if we swing by to collect my future intended?"

170

"As long as the conversation stays away from criminal proceedings."

"What'd Harriet say?"

"Oh, you know women. She wants to powder her nose and shower off the stench of corpses."

"Thank heaven for that. There's nothing like a shiny proboscis to take all the glamour out of a special occasion."

18

Finding a place to park, in what was once the capital of America's Wide Open Spaces, was always a challenge; but with another of Garth Brooks's comeback concerts bringing out the earlybirds to stand in line for four hours at the Hollywood Bowl, the Dodgers hosting the Yankees, the Tall Ships moored outside San Diego, and simultaneous demonstrations scheduled by PETA, Amnesty International, and the North American Coalition to Preserve and Protect the Leopard-Throated Snail, the entire L.A. basin looked like the employee lot at Microsoft. The two couples bailed out at a thirty-minute meter fifteen blocks from West Hollywood and The Oracle.

Valentino, veteran that he was, directed Harriet to remove a Jiffy peanut butter jar filled with quarters from the glove compartment.

"What am I supposed to do with this?"

she asked. "Brain the meter maid?"

"I thought we could set up a relay system to keep the kitty fed."

Broadhead reached over from the backseat, snatched the jar from her, got out, and hailed a curly headed Hispanic youth seated on the curb next to a sandwich board reading MAPS TO THE STARS HOMES $5.00. He gave the boy twenty dollars for four maps, handed him the jar, and said he'd buy four more for his friends among the college faculty if he'd crank a quarter into the slot every five minutes.

"Are you sure you can trust him?" Valentino asked as they began hiking.

"Why not? He looks just like that kid in *The Courtship of Eddie's Father.*"

Fanta said, "Who?"

The women were dressed practically, in leather walking shoes, slacks, and plain blouses, with the standard survival gear of water bottles, Gatorade, and chewing gum in their oversize shoulder bags. Broadhead, in heavy brown wingtips, thick tweeds, and his immigrant's cloth cap, was hobbling and sweating after two blocks; they stopped frequently while he caught his wind. Valentino took off his corduroy jacket and tied it around his waist.

"You look cute in a skirt," Harriet said.

173

"I'm secure enough to take that as a compliment, coming from a woman in pants."

Peter, the electrician, was waiting for them in front of the theater. He seized a cord attached to the heavy-duty cover he'd draped over the exposed wires in the marquee, and when they were all gathered on the sidewalk, tugged it loose. The cover fell away like the veil from a statue.

"He's one of you," Broadhead told Valentino. But even his tones were hushed.

Far above them, seeming to pierce the overlay of ocher smog spread like a dirty umbrella above the sprawling city, glittered a tower of thousands of LED lights, unlit at present, but reflecting what sunlight there was from their crystalline bulbs like scattered rhinestones.

Now it was Valentino's turn to express cynicism. "It looks okay, but what happens when the sun goes down?"

"I tested all the circuits," Peter said. "What happened, one of my crew mixed up the Load and Line wires. There are only four of each, but the mathematical combinations are almost endless. It was trial-and-error and a lot of testing and tagging to avoid repeating the same mistakes." With a flourish, the cheerful black technician drew

174

the remote control from the tool belt girdling his hips and gave it to his client.

Harriet pressed in close, taking Valentino's arm with both hands. He glanced sideways at his friends and saw with satisfaction that the fingers of the professor's right hand were interlaced with those of his fiancée's left.

"I'd say, 'Here goes nothing,' but that's what happened last time." He pressed the yellow button.

A geyser of brilliant electric light shot up the obelisk-shaped tower on all four sides and across the half-circle that sheltered the entrance like a cliff: a dazzling rainbow with the white lights bordering it chasing around the edges in a synchronized stutter of brilliant illumination.

The audience stared, as at a spectacular display of fireworks. Valentino felt light-headed. After all these years, the completion of his Sisyphean task seemed within sight.

Now all he had to worry about were the roof, the floors, the walls, and the disturbing noises made by whatever had taken up residence inside the ceiling over the snack bar.

Broadhead was the first to overcome his awe. "Just what was missing from Southern

California. Plenty of flash and no substance."

Fanta bent a knee, kicking the calf of his leg. "Me, too, you old goat. Let's go back to my place and make love."

"After I soak my feet."

"Congratulations, Val." Harriet raised her face. He kissed it, and turned to accept Peter's outstretched hand. He brought it back holding the electrician's bill.

There was a flurry of media activity once it was announced that the police had a person of interest in what the tabloid outlets had tagged "the Bombshell Murders;" no one now accepted the pretense that Karen Ogilvie had taken her own life. Whenever the story had lagged for want of a new development, the press had only to dig into the morgue files and rehash the details of the mysterious violent deaths of Thelma Todd, Marilyn Monroe, and Jayne Mansfield in Sunday magazine spreads chock-a-block with the cheesecake photos beloved of the genre.

"Also the same misinformation that was dished up as news the first time around," Broadhead pointed out.

With the shackles flung off, the paleontologists of the press broadened their excavations to include such non-related scandals as the Fatty Arbuckle trial following the sordid death of an obscure female guest at one of the silent comedian's wild parties and the still-unsolved murder of silent-film director William Desmond Taylor, complete with all the breathless myths that had been expounded at the time of the atrocities. The absence of a brazen blond star from those incidents was lost in the frenzy. (Roger Corman, rumor had it, was seeking the exclusive right to adapt the story to the screen.)

Sharing the projection booth/apartment with Valentino one evening three weeks into the investigation, Harriet Johansen put down the post-mortem photos she was studying with a magnifying lens to contemplate his troubled face. He happened to be looking at a TV commercial for a local used-car dealership, but it was clear from his expression he was still immersed in *Entertainment Tonight*'s most recent feature, a mishmash of sound bite interviews with red-carpet celebrities who knew no more about the murders than anyone watching from his living room, but all of whom seemed to have definite opinions on the subject.

"You know, Val, the organization I work for does get it right most of the time.

Sheridan's said nothing to draw suspicion away from him."

"He hasn't confessed, either. Padilla was confident he would any minute."

"A show of confidence is a cop's best weapon. Most murderers are familiar with their victims, and everything about this case points to a personal connection."

"What's personal about waiting someone's table?"

"I'm talking about Sheridan and Root. I'm not assigned to this one, so I can't form an opinion on whether Padilla was right about the others. But he was dead-on about Sheridan inheriting everything upon his partner's death. Root had no other bequests in his will, and he didn't have a chance to change it between the time he quarreled with Sheridan and he was murdered."

"You never met Sheridan. I'll need more than a strong motive to convince me he was acting."

"He probably wasn't. Most killers regret their actions. And you have to agree there have been no other such killings since Sheridan's been in custody."

"This one's clever, Harriet. Too clever to bring the heat back down on him while he's got a pigeon filling in for him."

"I've worked some serial cases. These

people don't kill just because they enjoy it. They do it because they can't stop themselves. Based on the cycles so far, he'd have acted again long before this."

"Maybe he skipped town. Do you keep up with investigations outside this jurisdiction?"

"Not usually. I'm not that much of a workaholic. But because you're involved — interested, I should say — I've paid close attention to the heads-up stuff the FBI feeds the department daily. Their only person of interest in some serial homicides in Maryland is a white-haired widow who knows more about commonly available poisons than is good for those who come into contact with her. The rest is the usual terrorist stuff. Unless your phantom maniac has been misreading the Koran or has redirected his attention from bombshell blondes to postmen and census-takers, in my professional opinion the LAPD's on the right track and you're obsessing over something more than old movies. I prefer you prattling on about John Wayne than John Wayne Gacy."

"You're right, of course." He picked up the remote and switched to *Wheel of Fortune.*

"Good." She returned to her study of a

severed larynx.

"Unless," he said, watching Vanna White flip over letters, "our killer isn't a nut."

She started to groan; then slid the photo back into the file and took off her reading glasses. "What do you mean by that?"

He turned off the set and leaned forward, dangling the remote between his knees. "What if our killer isn't insane?"

"The odds are he isn't; or at least not the way usually associated with mass murderers. Padilla's theory is —"

"— that Sheridan cobbled up a serial pattern in order to divert attention from his real purpose, which was to kill his partner in order to ensure his security. Everyone assumes it had to be one or the other. No one's considered a third possibility, that there's a Mr. X acting on a motive we haven't even thought of."

"Which brings us back to your mysterious projectionist. The lieutenant and I are colleagues," she said. "I'll find out if he's been working that angle. He has, you know. What he said's true: No good detective stops detecting just because he's got a good suspect in the cage."

"I'd like to be in on that meeting."

"What, you don't trust me?"

"You're the only person in this world I

trust completely. If it turns out he's wrong, I want to hear him admit it to my face."

"If he isn't — and I'm sure he's not, he's one of the best we have — you realize you'd be giving him another chance to make fun of you for playing detective."

"He'd have that right. I'm not the easily bruised creature you think."

"You are, though; which is one of the reasons I love spending time with you. I spend most of my day with hard-hearted cynics. It's their way of coping with the dregs of humanity they spend most of *their* days among. Here's the deal: If I ask him about those projectionists and he says nothing came of that line, you drop this matter and don't mention it again."

"You think that by not talking about it I'll stop thinking about it?"

"I think that you're a reasonable person, who understands that when there's no other place to look, you've found what you were after, and won't let it keep eating you."

"That's not fair."

"What's not fair?"

"Drawing the 'reasonable' card."

And he smiled. After a second, she returned the expression and put her glasses back on.

"The jig's up."

"What?" She started, looking up from the file.

Valentino was watching *Wheel of Fortune*. " 'The jig's up,' " he repeated, gesturing toward the half-finished puzzle on-screen. "Phrase."

"You're hopeless."

"If I were, we wouldn't be having this conversation."

19

The next day was a Saturday. It being Harriet's day off, Valentino didn't begrudge her postponing their meeting with Padilla until Monday. They attended the Garth Brooks concert: Her section chief had given her tickets when his wife went into labor three weeks early. Neither of them was particularly fond of modern country music, but it was a rare social evening out, and to turn down her superior's generosity would not have served her career well.

They enjoyed themselves tremendously. The artist was at the top of his form after his long and highly praised hiatus to throw over fame and glory to spend time with family, and even Broadhead, who caught the concert on cable, remarked that it was refreshing to listen to music with a discernible melody and understandable lyrics. ("There isn't a true rhyme in a carload; but one can't have everything.") The couple fed off the enthusiasm of a manic audience and found themselves humming the star's signature tunes while waiting for the parking lot to clear.

Valentino spent Sunday with Broadhead in the Film Preservation Department's screening room, viewing the jumpy frames of a 1915 silent adaptation of *Much Ado About Nothing,* recently discovered in of all places, a bomb shelter in a previously top-secret Soviet training facility in Siberia. They had to admit, despite doubts about the Bard's immortal poetry being reduced to actors' face-making and scraps of dialogue consigned to title cards, that there was a certain advantage in being able to fill in the many continuity gaps with the help of the Folger Library, and looked forward to the funds that would be siphoned off from art-house showings into the department's treasury.

"Who knows?" grumped Broadhead. "We might scrape together enough rubles to remaster *Scudda Hoo, Scudda Hey!*"

Valentino, preoccupied with what the morrow might bring, dismissed his mentor's sarcasm as a symptom of his fast-approaching nuptials. Despite his loathing of all things hackneyed, Broadhead had agreed to a June wedding. His bride-to-be, for all her rebellious attitude, was a traditionalist at heart.

"I was married the first time in December," he comforted himself aloud, "which brought a whole new terror to the first sighting of a sidewalk Santa at Halloween."

"I thought it was a happy marriage," said Valentino, who had never known the first Mrs. Broadhead.

"It was. The thought that there might be *two* women who would tolerate my constant presence is a source of humility and awe. I'll remind you of this as your tenth anniversary approaches, and you find yourself having to outdo the previous nine. The pressure mounts exponentially."

At this point his friend changed the subject by directing attention to the grainy image on-screen. Valentino and Harriet had yet to discuss the possibility of a lifelong commitment, despite the assumption of everyone who knew them that the event was inevitable.

As it happened, when she called the next morning with a time and place for the date with Padilla, he'd forgotten all about it. Leo Kalishnikov, his theater designer, had presented him with his latest report of disaster: While digging up The Oracle's basement to replace sections of the brittle foundation, the excavating crew had struck water: a geyser, in fact, in the middle of the worst drought in the history of Southern California. New drainage tile would have to be laid, more permits arranged, and the cost "substantial." Which was a word Valentino had come to dread. "I could sugarcoat the details," the other told him, "but it wouldn't make them less grim."

The film archivist's life had broken into two separate parts: construction and criminal investigation. When the Russian called back with the welcome news that the water had come from a broken main only, whose repair would run a fraction of the amount anticipated, Valentino had forgotten about the basement. Harriet had called: They were to meet with the lieutenant on enemy ground: The Long Arm, a cocktail lounge three blocks from the Beverly Hills station, and a cop hangout so notorious not even a deadbeat dad had gone within a mile of it in years.

"What can I expect?" he'd asked. He'd seen enough of the real thing lately to know that the movies were unreliable on the subject.

"Oh, the usual: old prizefighting posters, bare electric bulbs, and over everything the distinct bouquet of Kentucky Rye."

"Now you're playing with me."

"Relax, darling. The owner sold all the spittoons for scrap years ago."

He arrived on time, and found Harriet seated alone in a well-lit booth upholstered in shiny green Naugahyde and neat paper napkins with THE LONG ARM embossed on them in block letters. Men and women, some in street clothes, others in uniform, sat at tables and around a bar overhung with crystal glasses in grooved racks, with a soccer game playing on flat-screen monitors. Something was trilling softly over a concealed sound system. Valentino strained to make it out: "Walk On By."

"I've turned down three drinks sent to me by three different patrons," Harriet said, raising her face for a peck. "One of them was kind of cute."

"The patron or the drink?"

"The patron. He runs the records bureau in Huntington Park."

"He probably just wanted to dust you for prints."

He couldn't blame the others. She was beautiful even in the shapeless smock she wore to work, more so once she'd changed into a sleeveless blouse and skirt. She watched him closely as he sat down across from her, looking around. "Disappointed?"

"A little. The place might as well be an Olive Garden."

"Don't be taken in by the ambience. Last year a couple of punks in ski masks stuck a shotgun in the bartender's face and guess what happened?"

"I can hear actually hear the pistols cocking."

"It was like a fire crackling through Laurel Canyon. This is where every cop in the city comes to cash his paycheck. Even the bartender drew down on them. He retired from active duty when Detroit broke up the gang squad."

He looked at the man behind the bar, a mild-looking sixty in horn-rimmed glasses and a polka-dot bow tie. "Where's our host?"

"He isn't buying, we are. This was our idea, remember? Be patient. He's only a couple of minutes late."

They ordered drinks: white wine for her, a Miller Lite for him. He'd nurse it; two beers and he was no good for the rest of the day. But a Dr Pepper seemed inappropriate to the expected company.

Padilla came in just as the bartender was setting out their drinks, nodding here and there to scattered patrons. He wore the same conservative suit. Valentino wondered what had become of his distinctive double-knits. The laws of the State of California would prohibit disposing of them in public landfills because of what they might do to the water table, and burning them would have sent up a signal flame visible from outer space. The newcomer plunked himself down beside Harriet. "Diet Pepsi," he told the bartender.

Valentino goggled. The lieutenant smiled bitterly and held up a colorful plastic chip. "Five years sober." He put it away. "It was the Scotch or the job."

Padilla was opening up, it seemed. Valentino began to feel less on edge.

The other produced his wallet, as if he were going to pony up for all their drinks after all, but instead of bills drew out three business cards.

"You were right about Limerick, Ogilvie, and Root: Stone pros, respecting the rules of the projectionists' union."

"So you have a new suspect?" He tried to keep the eagerness from his tone.

"See for yourself."

Valentino accepted the cards. The first read:

S. A. BRUGH
PROJECTIONIST
A.S.M.P.T.

"American Society of Motion Picture Technicians," he said. "One of the biggest unions in the industry, and one of the most powerful."

"So he told me."

The next contained the same information under the name Bernard Schwartz.

Without comment, Valentino looked at the third. The identical legends, but this time the name was Mike Morrison.

"Three different guys," Padilla said. "But they all had to belong to the union. I interviewed Brugh. My team tracked down Schwartz and Morrison. Brugh had run Limerick's projector from time to time — it's in company records — and Schwartz and Morrison had each done the same for Ogilvie and Root. The last two had dicey alibis: Schwartz said he was walking his dog in his Orange County neighborhood around the time the CSIs figure Ogilvie was killed; two of his neighbors thought they saw him, but since he walked the dog just about every night at that time they couldn't swear if it was *that* night. Morrison went to a movie — if you can believe that, what he does for a living — alone. There were no ushers and the ticket clerk never looks at faces."

"What about Brugh?"

"He was scheduled to work the projector

the day Limerick wanted to screen that picture for you — the day you found her body — but then he got a message through his company canceling the gig. That was an hour before he was expected. After he got word he went to his ex-wife's place in Long Beach and borrowed his kid. They rented a sloop and went sailing all day. The ex, the boy, and the guy who rents boats at the marina backed him up."

"How hard did you lean on the others?"

Padilla snatched back the cards.

"We don't lean. We persevere. My crew, which I trained myself, is satisfied neither one of them is Jack the Ripper. If we didn't have a suspect as sweet as Sheridan, we might risk a harassment suit and press 'em tight, but I got people to answer to, and if you think the rank of lieutenant means job security, you know even less about police than the guys who write movies. You can't blast a captain out of his spot, and sergeant's too low in the order to look like anything but a scapegoat; the press can smell a cover-up like that a mile away. Scrapping a lieutenant spins nice on the six o'clock news, and there's always a line of good men and women waiting to take his place.

"Plus," he said, "we got a confession from Sheridan."

The bartender brought Padilla's Pepsi. He returned the business cards to his wallet, sipped, and studied Valentino's face. Turning to Harriet, he said, "I got through finally. I was starting to think it would take a massive stroke to make your boyfriend go up in his lines."

Valentino drank beer. It tasted as bitter as the lieutenant's smile.

■ ■ ■ ■

III
THE FEARLESS
VAMPIRE KILLERS

■ ■ ■ ■

20

By mercy of events, Valentino found distance from sordid things in the flurry of his closest friend's nuptials; the fittings for the bridegroom's raiment continued apace, as did the arrangements for the ceremony itself, most of which fell to Harriet, as maid of honor; earlier incidents involving the acquisition of Red Montana's first cowboy feature had put the details of the bachelor party months in the past. For all the bride's millennial-charged chiding, and the groom's relentless curmudgeonism, Fanta and Kyle were a match made, if not exactly in heaven, then certainly in the fairy-tale atmosphere of Hollywood, remote island that it was in the sea of twenty-first-century reality.

The professor, who'd lost touch with his only progeny sometime in the turgid sixties (a son, Valentino gathered; but whose circumstances were as plainly *verboten* to inquiry as the father's mysterious incarceration in Communist Yugoslavia), had no interest in propagation, and the legal student had made her peace (with relief, it seemed), with the diagnosis that she was incapable of reproducing. That hurdle overcome, the difference in their generations was entirely a matter of their own discussion.

The future wedding party experienced an ominous preview of fireworks to come when the bride-to-be asked Harriet to attend the cake tasting.

The maid of honor demurred. "I'm trying to watch my waistline. I can just fit into that horrible dress you picked out. Anyway, isn't that the groom's responsibility?"

Fanta looked like the poster child for bridal jitters. "Please? The old bear blew up when I asked him. He said, 'What's the point? Every wedding cake tastes the same: melted cotton candy poured over a Hostess Sno Ball. It should come with a shot of insulin.' "

"You know, he's kind of right," said Valentino, when the telephone conversation was reported to him.

"Not the point. If I have to go, so do you."

The room, usually reserved for private parties, was closed off from the others in the Culver City patisserie. It wasn't enough that Fanta and Harriet had to sample the various wedges presented by the female proprietor, a sturdy brunette with jet-trail eyebrows like Vampira; he was obliged to pick up a fork as well. The first tasted exactly as Broadhead had described it, the second something like Bazooka bubble gum. He was lifting a forkful of the third when the bridegroom entered, scarlet-faced and wearing his tweed Ellis Island uniform.

"You came!" Fanta's eyes sparkled.

He stopped in his tracks before their table. "I thought by now you'd have moved on to the figures for the top of the cake."

"That comes later. What are you hiding behind your back?"

He brought his hand around in front of him and opened it. A green ceramic frog glistened on his palm.

The sparkle faded. "Which one is it?"

"The groom, of course."

"If that's how you see us, we need counseling."

The others excused themselves. Outside, Valentino expelled a gust of air. "I can't wait for what happens after the honeymoon, the first time they discuss whether to watch *The Seventh Seal* or *Hot Tub Time Machine.*"

The look Harriet gave him was not unlike what Broadhead had gotten from Fanta. "You can't visualize them working out their difficulties in bed, can you?"

His response was to turn Technicolor red; but he attempted to pose as a man of the world. "I'm sure he picked up some things during his travels abroad. You know, there's a showing of *Metropolis* tonight at Grauman's. The department played a part in the reconstruction. Are you up for it?"

"You know, you won't always be able to depend on old Hollywood to redirect the course of an uncomfortable conversation."

They were stopped at a red light. He leaned in as close as he could against the restraint of his seat belt. "I'll buy the refreshments. I'll even pop for those pretzel bites you can't resist."

"Uh-huh. I'll meet you halfway. AMC is running *The Breakfast Club* continuously starting at eight P.M. We can catch the first showing and fight over the relative merits of Molly Ringwald and Brigitte Helm over dinner at the Morocco Lounge."

"The Morocco? I was thinking of a quick sandwich at the Brass Gimbal on the way home."

"As good as the James Wong Howe Chop Suey sounds, I thought the Rack of Lamb Nelson Mandela a bit more suited to our second anniversary."

Which hit him like a runaway piano in a

Hal Roach feature. He couldn't believe two years had passed since they'd met; and since he'd sunk himself in the mire of bringing The Oracle back to its former glory.

The Morocco was one of the few dining spots in L.A. where a dress code was enforced. The effect Harriet had upon the male clientele, wearing a frost-green off-the-shoulder cocktail dress and the emerald earrings Valentino had given her on her last birthday (putting off the purchase of platinum doorknobs), made him grateful for his decision to have his one-and-only suit dry-cleaned and pressed. She'd approved, making one adjustment only: jettisoning the necktie printed with megaphones and movie cameras in favor of a gift provided by her, a shimmering silk tie that matched her dress.

A rarity in a culture that celebrated departed glory, the establishment contained no references, visual or otherwise, to extinct Hollywood. Instead it opted for Manhattan elegance. The maitre d' wore tails, the waiters short red jackets with brass buttons, and one could cut a finger on the creases in the crisp linen tablecloths. There were no potted palms, no beaded curtains, and the pianist sat at a glistening black baby grand playing selections from light opera. In their well-meaning effort to blast the Tinseltown stereotype, the restaurant's designers had substituted someone else's vision for home-grown originality.

"What are you looking for?" asked Harriet, once her chair had been pulled out for her and they were seated.

Valentino stopped craning his neck. "Noël Coward; or a reasonable facsimile." He caught her expression. "I'm sorry. It tries so hard not to look like the movies it looks like a set from *Top Hat.*"

"You know, Val, I don't mind your pet obsession. In fact, it's one of the things that attracted me to you in the first place. The men I was involved with before you were all so relentlessly grown up — lawyers, investment brokers, insurance actuaries, whatever those are — your childish infatuation with make-believe was like a blast of fresh air. I indulged that, I admit; but when you apply the movies to every experience we share —"

"Say no more." He smiled, propped an elbow on the table, and held out his hand. To his relief, she laid hers in it without hesitation. "In my defense, they're no less important to me, or to my livelihood, than legal precedents, the prime rate, and how long a client is expected to live — that's what an actuary does, by the way — but sometimes I make the mistake of defining myself by my work. Also this murder case refuses to leave my mind. I'll try to do better."

She smiled in turn and squeezed his hand. "What's that line from *How to Lose a Guy in Ten Days?* Oh, yes: 'Bullshit.' That's not all that's worrying you. Every time the subject of our friends' wedding comes up, you go deeper into *Merton of the Movies.* Is it us you're worried about?"

"No. Well, not us, particularly. Well, us."

She slid her hand out of his. His heart fell; but then he saw the red-jacketed waiter approaching their table. They ordered drinks and found themselves alone again.

"That thing between Kyle and Fanta works for them," he said. "That whole Tracy-Hepburn friction thing. I don't want us to be like that."

"We won't be. For one thing, you and I were born only two months apart. That May–December whatever is a scene from another movie; there I go, rationalizing things on your terms. Don't you realize I wouldn't make the attempt if I weren't crazy about you — baby?"

He flushed. "Do me a favor and don't quote from *Double Indemnity* when you're trying to get me into bed."

They were interrupted again, but this time

there was no scarlet coat. The sight of Lieutenant Ray Padilla approaching their table, looking as uncomfortable as ever in tasteful gray worsted, the uniform of established authority, catapulted the scene straight out of romantic comedy back into murder melodrama.

"This a private party, or can I barge in?"

"Would it make a difference if I said no?" But Valentino was relieved by the distraction. He didn't fear commitment so much as the question whether he could support both a marriage and The Oracle, and the prospect of being forced to choose between them shattered any chance of his ever having another good night's sleep.

Without answering, the newcomer appropriated a chair from a vacant table, sat, and scooted it up to theirs. He stuck a thumb back over his shoulder. "Twenty-second anniversary."

"Won't she be annoyed you left her?" It seemed he couldn't escape the subject of matrimony.

"She's in the powder room. I don't know what they do in there and I don't want to, but she's good for twenty minutes. Sitting there alone with all that texting going on around me gives me the hives. Sounds like a flock of woodpeckers on crack. Hello,

Johansen."

"Hello, Ray. Why do you only use last names? You sound like a boardroom cartoon in *The New Yorker.*"

"I lost two partners within a day after I started calling them by their first names. A shooting and a heart attack. Not that I'm superstitious." He rapped his knuckles on the table and shifted his attention to Valentino. "I'm still working that projectionist angle. You didn't think I forgot it, did you?"

"No, but I thought you were satisfied with your suspect's confession."

"I never liked it. Some guys got only so much fight in 'em, then they throw in the towel 'cause they feel guilty about some failure in the relationship. When the cell door slams shut they get second thoughts, and out goes the confession. I got to do the legwork anyway, so why not now? Maybe it's nothing, but the only Social Security number we matched to a name on our list of projectionists the victims hired belonged to Brugh, the first one."

"What were the other names again?"

Padilla produced his notebook, which had fallen further apart since the last time. "Bernard Schwartz and Mike Morrison. The union issued them both cards, but like most places they never bothered to validate the government numbers. That kind of thing only comes back months later, with a query from Washington; if at all. Right now the bureaucrats have got their hands full with affordable health care, what part of it's deductible and what isn't. It only came to light this time because like I said, I keep my briefs covered in court."

"That's clever," Harriet said. "I didn't know you had a sense of humor."

"And you call yourself a cop?"

"I'm not a cop. You watch too much television. They don't give me a badge or a gun, and if they catch me in the same room with a real-live suspect, it better be a co-incidence."

"I'll put it this way: If I didn't know a good joke when I heard it, you might as well start calling me by my first name right now, 'cause without it I'd put a slug in my skull."

Valentino said, "Hold on. Going back to the subject of first names, what was Brugh's?"

Notebook. "Said S. A. on the card. We got the rest from his union file." He used both thumbs to turn pages hanging on by one or two holes to the spiral without losing them, stopped, grunted. "No wonder he goes by his initials. He must be good with his dukes or he'd never have survived grammar school

204

with that moniker. Spangler Arlington. Pipe that, will you? Spangler Arlington Brugh."

Valentino looked at Harriet, but got nothing back. *Well,* he thought, *you can't tell someone everything you know in just two years.*

"Lieutenant," he said, "I think you should consider releasing Eleazar Sheridan."

21

Their waiter came with their drinks. Padilla handed him a credit card. "Settle their bill; mine, too. I'm seated over there." Once again he jerked his thumb back over his shoulder.

"We haven't eaten," Valentino said.

"At the rate this joint moves, you'll starve to death before they bring out the artichoke dip. Hang on, I'll call a cab and send my wife home." He pushed back his chair and left them.

"This is one anniversary she'll remember," Harriet said. "Him, too."

"I'll say it to you before he says it to her: Sorry about dinner."

"That's okay. I've always wondered where a man like Ray Padilla gets all his energy."

The lieutenant and the waiter returned at the same time; the couple barely had time for one sip. The shade of red in Padilla's face told them how the domestic conversation had gone. He signed the receipt and they went out.

"Blue Chevy." He gave the valet his ticket. "We'll come back for your car."

Valentino asked where they were going.

"Best barbecue in town, and fast: in and out in fifteen minutes."

"With or without bicarb?" Harriet asked.

The lieutenant drove fast, cutting in and out of traffic, passing fenders nearly close enough to skin off the top coat of paint.

"If you're in a hurry, why not use the siren?" Valentino asked.

"Don't have one. It's my personal car."

His passenger consoled himself with Padilla's story about patrolling Watts in a squad car; without professional skill, all they had to depend on was luck. On Central Avenue he swung into the curb down the block from a grimy brick building with a neon pig on the roof wearing a chef's hat and waving a fork.

Harriet said, "That's a deeply disturbing image."

Padilla grunted. "I'd tell 'em to change the sign, but then the place might catch on. First you need to make a reservation a year ahead, then they start pouring the sauce from a jar."

The inside was garishly lit, with a low

plaster ceiling and a visible path worn in the linoleum between the swinging door leading into the kitchen and the serving area. The air was so thick with fried onion Valentino's eyes streamed water. Only half the tables were occupied during the dinner hour. Their menu was printed on plastic place mats stuck to the laminate with something that wasn't glue.

A chunky Mexican in a dirty apron — the proprietor, most likely — served them pulled-pork sandwiches, coleslaw, and Pepsi fizzing in waxed cups bearing the image of the porcine cannibal. The buns were glazed, irregular in size, and obviously baked on the premises.

"It's delicious!" Harriet wiped her mouth with a brown paper towel torn off the roll on the table.

"Yeah. They start smoking it in the parking lot in back at sunup and don't open till six P.M. I'm taking Grace here next year."

"Better make it tomorrow night," she said.

"This isn't the first time I disappointed her; but yeah." He took a bite and swallowed. "Spill it, Ebert. What makes Sheridan innocent all of a sudden?"

Valentino ate. The meat was so tender he found chewing unnecessary. "The names of those projectionists. I should say, '*the* projectionist.' Bernard Schwartz. Mike Morrison."

"You left out Brugh."

"I did that on purpose. Brugh's the only one who gave you his real name."

"Get to the point. You're slower than the Morocco Lounge."

"I should have seen it the first time you mentioned the names, but Bernard Schwartz is fairly common and I'm sure there are other Mike Morrisons. S. A. Brugh didn't ring any bells, but when you told me what the initials stood for, I couldn't miss it. There could have been only one other Spangler Arlington Brugh. That one changed it when he went into acting. The world knew him best as Robert Taylor."

"I know that one. I've seen reruns of *The Detectives.*"

"He was around a long time before that. He acted opposite Greta Garbo in *Camille* in 1936. *This* Brugh's parents may have been related, or just knew Taylor's story because they happened to have the same last name, and thought it would be appropriate when they christened their child."

"Okay so far. What about the others?"

"Other, period. Tony Curtis was born Bernard Schwartz, and Marion Michael Morrison took the name John Wayne when he came to Hollywood. One projectionist who shares his name with a movie star is co-incidence enough without believing two others, both belonging to the same union."

"But we interviewed them."

Harriet pointed at him with a forkful of coleslaw. "You said you interviewed Brugh, but others talked to Schwartz and Morrison. Why should they suspect they were talking to the same man?"

"So how come Brugh's not a suspect?"

Valentino said, "It's easy enough to confirm he goes by his real name. He had a strong alibi for the time of Beata Limerick's murder. What if another projectionist took his place, using his name to get in the door? We already know he's familiar with industry legend. He must have been aware of the Taylor connection. Passing himself off as Brugh the first time is what gave him the idea to use other stars' original names to get close enough to Karen Ogilvie and Geoffrey Root to kill them."

"Why did Sheridan say he killed Root?" Harriet asked.

"Lieutenant?"

Padilla gurgled the last of his Pepsi through the straw. "I already said I didn't like it. I told you before that sensitive type doesn't break as easy as a tough guy. When they do, it's usually because they don't have the strength to go on denying it. I can usually smell a phony confession, but when a case involves so many people connected with the acting racket, I get to doubting my own instincts."

Valentino said, "Let's assume the victims all called the union asking for the services of a professional projectionist. Say our man belongs, keeps in constant touch with the office, and takes the assignments he wants — meaning those involving the clients he intends to murder — so someone else doesn't beat him to the job. He's probably registered under those other two names, so if he did come up with that scheme after substituting for the real Brugh, it means he's signed up recently. You need to concentrate on late joiners whose references were accepted without checking. It happens, especially when whoever's in charge of registration is swamped."

"Which would likely be the case with a projectionists' union in L.A." Padilla scowled at his half-eaten sandwich.

"There is a flaw in the theory," Valentino said. "Is an insane serial killer capable of that kind of planning?"

Harriet said, "Any forensics expert can tell you there are two kinds of serials, organized and random. The second kind wanders around until it stumbles on a convenient victim, then acts on impulse. That was Son of Sam, following the voices in his head. The first stalks his prey, sometimes for days or weeks or months, and sets an elaborate trap. That was Ted Bundy: His IQ was off the charts."

"There's another kind."

She looked at Padilla. "Everything I've read says there are just the two."

"I'm talking about a serial who isn't a nutcase. One with a clear motive and field experience who gets away with it longer than most because everyone's out looking for Jack the Ripper when they should be looking for Pittsburgh Phil."

"Who's Pittsburgh Phil?" Valentino asked.

The lieutenant's smile was grim. "Here's where *I* get to be the buff. He was the most successful hit man in the history of Murder, Incorporated."

22

Dessert came, a mound of fried ice cream the size of a monkey's head, with ground cashews sprinkled on top and a dark-chocolate candy bar embedded inside, to go off like a sweet bomb when one discovered it, with a blast of euphoria Valentino assumed was similar to a rush of cocaine. It was delicious and absolutely lethal.

Padilla, it developed, had a sweet tooth. He finished half his portion before he resumed speaking. "There isn't a thing about this case I like. Normally, the odds are with the house: Murders are committed by and large by amateurs; we deal with it on a regular basis and know all the things the perp never thought of, including the bright ideas he got about pulling off the perfect crime. Serial killers screw up the routine; their motives make sense only to them, and since they don't have any sense to begin with, we're always a step behind waiting for a break, or until somebody catches 'em in the act. The professionals, on the other hand, know as much about the act as we do, if they're any good at it and have experience. That adds another whole step: We have to find out who hired 'em and what *his* motives are."

"What makes this one special?" Harriet asked. "Serial killings have gotten to be as common as earthquakes in Asia, and hit men have been around as long as the Mafia; long enough anyway to call for a protocol all its own."

"What makes this one special is for the first time in my career I've got to depend on a civilian for input. The only reason I'm telling all this to one is his girlfriend's a colleague, kind of."

"Thank you so much."

"Forget it." Nothing about the lieutenant's response suggested he was aware of the sarcasm in Harriet's tone. "Anyway that's why I'm sharing stuff we generally sit on till it hatches." With a noise that coming from anyone else Valentino would have called a sigh, Padilla left a spoonful of half-melted frozen sugar, egg, vanilla extract, and salt in the bottom of his bowl and shoved it away. "I'm kicking Sheridan. My chief won't like it, but when you're doing a jigsaw puzzle and you have to carve away at a piece to make it fit, the picture won't work." He looked at Valentino, and if the film archivist didn't know better he might have thought there was a touch of respect in his expression. "That movie-star-name angle's as nuts as the cashews I got chewing holes in my diverticulosis, but I probably wouldn't have stumbled on it on my own. If James Stewart shows up, I'll know I'm on the right track."

"James Stewart?" He combed his knowledge of cinema history and came up empty.

Grinning, the Homicide detective glanced at the bill, took out his wallet, and started counting bills. A sign on the door to the restaurant read: CREDIT'S WHAT YOU GET WHEN YOU'RE DEAD. WE ACCEPT ALL KINDS OF CASH. "You don't have the corner, Siskel. James Stewart was Stewart Granger's real name. The swashbuckler? He couldn't use it on account of it was already taken."

"What do you think of that?" Valentino asked Harriet, as their host approached the cash register.

"I think that's a very troubled man. He had to throw aside everything he learned the hard way and fight by your rules."

LAPD LAYS AN EGG, ran the headline in *Variety,* when Eleazar Sheridan's release was

215

announced. Kyle Broadhead snapped shut his copy and slapped it down on top of the pile of pages he'd accumulated on his treatise on movie history and theory, his magnum opus based on a half-century of research. "The vultures are feeding on themselves now. It was fresh when they said the same thing about Wall Street in 'twenty-nine."

Valentino couldn't help himself. "How much did you lose on that deal?"

"I threw myself out of a window in the Empire State Building; I thought that was common knowledge. Just how old do you think I am?"

"That's the bonus question in *Who Wants to Be a Millionaire.* The office pool is up to five hundred. I've got the slot between the signing of the Magna Carta and Truman's second term."

Broadhead scowled at the African violet flourishing in a pot on his otherwise Spartan desk. The plant was a gift from Fanta, who'd challenged him to keep it alive. Taking up the gauntlet, he'd stashed a garden trowel, a pair of canvas gloves, and a sack of Miracle-Gro in the kneehole, amassed a botanical library to rival Luther Burbank's, and fussed about grubs, Japanese beetles, and fungal blight with all the passion he brought to the seminal works of the cinema pioneers of turn-of-the-century France. If Valentino weren't convinced his mentor considered his own past of less import than the history of film, he'd have accused him of trying to compensate for his own failures as a father to his estranged son. As it was, he considered this sudden passion positive evidence of his dedication to his forthcoming marriage.

Valentino just hoped that Fanta herself hadn't become lost in his attention to the institution. Certainly the old man, for all his labors on behalf of the art of the motion picture, seemed to take little pleasure from just watching a movie for its own sake. In that, the master and the student stood on opposite sides of an unbridgeable chasm.

What the master said next caught him by surprise.

"Is it grotesque I'm marrying a girl half the age of my Ph.D.?"

Valentino hesitated. "That's not my call, Kyle. I can't believe you two haven't discussed the situation." He wouldn't say it to his friend, but it was the eight-hundred-pound gorilla in every water-cooler conversation surrounding the match.

"*I* have; *she* won't. Every time I bring it up she changes the subject. Is she ducking

217

it, do you think?"

"I can't picture Fanta ducking anything. Next to Harriet she's the most take-charge woman I've ever met."

"You're forgetting someone else."

He knew immediately to whom Broadhead was referring. "Thank God she hasn't reared her head this time."

Simultaneously they knocked wood.

"I don't see the problem," Valentino said then. "One of you with reservations is one thing, both another. If Fanta thought the generation gap was a problem, she'd have brought it up before now. She's studying for the bar. They don't face the exam without evaluating all the issues. In any case, you should discuss it. You didn't become the head of the department, and twist as many arms as you've had to in order to squeeze donations out of those stones you corner at cocktail parties, by backing away from a fight."

"Which is another of those differences I have difficulty overcoming. Youth thinks it has all the answers."

He let that drift. One of the drawbacks of flying a permanent orbit around old movies was the persistent need to apologize to the people one dealt with for his date of birth.

"Maybe it's pre-wedding jitters," Broadhead said. "A man gets set in his ways. What if she's the kind who wants to rearrange the furniture all the time? One night I might take a flying leap into bed, hit a bare patch of floor, and wind up on life support."

Valentino laughed. "I wouldn't worry about that. She'll probably put you into cardiac arrest on your wedding night."

"That's where you're wrong. I made an appointment for a complete physical the day I proposed — or to be honest, the day she proposed to me. My doctor says I'll live to be a hundred if I don't fall into an open manhole."

"Your doctor weighs three hundred pounds and smokes three packs a day."

"Why do you think he's my doctor?"

Ruth entered without knocking. Such amenities had dwindled away from her past working method in dealing with the last of the old studio moguls, if she'd ever observed them in the first place. "You've got a call," she told Valentino. "You want me to transfer it to this line?" She made it sound as if expecting him to conduct business of any sort was an open question. He'd long since given up trying to convince her that preserving film classics was a real profession.

"Who is it?"

"She wouldn't leave her name."

He told her to go ahead, and she withdrew without another word. When the light on Broadhead's phone came on he answered. His colleague perked up at his tone.

"If you must know, yes, I'm trying to help out the department in my small way. What's your interest? Seriously? I can't answer that." The dial tone sounded in his ear. He hung up. "I'm never going to knock wood again."

"Really? Her?"

Valentino nodded. "Teddie Goodman, as I live and breathe. It was a fishing expedition. She thinks I'm stringing along the Los Angeles Police Department in order to beat Mark David Turkus to the punch. It must be hard work being Theodosia Goodman. When Iraq lobs a missile into Israel, she thinks Tel Aviv has a line on *The Thief of Baghdad*."

Turkus, the billionaire media baron who'd outbid the UCLA Film Preservation Department on more acquisitions than Valentino cared to remember, only put his ace sleuth on a project when he intended to play hardball. She was the third take-charge woman neither one of them had wanted to name, for fear of summoning the devil.

Broadhead blew air. "A thing like that can destroy one's faith in superstition. When that woman fishes, she packs a shotgun." His eyes narrowed. "You haven't been holding out on me, have you? Beata or Karen or Root didn't promise you the lost last reel from *Casablanca:* the one where Bogart runs off with Bergman, leaving Paul Henreid to face the Nazis alone?"

Valentino went stiff in his chair. "Such a thing exists?"

"Idiot. I was being ironic. Now you're the one ducking the issue."

"Don't be ridiculous. She waltzed all around her point; if there was the smallest doubt in her mind I didn't know what she was getting at, she wasn't about to give me anything I could get my teeth into. But if she's got the scent, the fact that there's something significant on the other end of her nose is something you can take to the bank."

23

Teddie Goodman exploded into Valentino's office less than forty-five minutes after she'd called. *Exploded* was no exaggeration. She swept through doors as if they didn't exist, wearing outfits one saw only in *Harper's Bazaar* the very day she appeared in them in public: Outlandish things that clove to her skeleton frame as closely as if she'd sloughed off the last, like a snake. This one, white with a scarlet spiral that put Valentino in mind of a barber's pole, culminated in a burst of crimson daffodil on her left shoulder, echoing the bloodred lipstick she wore in contrast to her black-black hair, swept behind one ear and lacquered tight to the temple.

Her name, as it happened, belonged to silent-screen vamp Theda Bara, before she'd sought fame. Valentino, who owed his own name to Bara's contemporary through an accident of birth, had sought to soft-pedal that connection by grooming himself more casually than the slick original, but Teddie seemed to spend an inordinate amount of time in replicating the slinky image of her namesake. She appeared to feel the necessity to feed her employer's romantic fantasies about early Hollywood. Considering her obvious skills in sniffing out forgotten gems, Valentino thought she must feel some deep-seated insecurity concerning her station; which was why he gave her more latitude than most.

"I'd sit," she said, looking around his office cluttered with scripts and related detritus, "but the place is a deathtrap. I might have to make for the fire stairs any minute."

"Good day to you, too, Teddie. To what do I owe the pleasure?"

"Can it, Sherlock. If you're so tight with the cops, it means you're snitching on someone for a quid pro quo. What've you got, Marilyn's testimony against the Kennedys on tape?"

He was surprised. Ordinarily he had a line on some item of interest to them both, but in this case his efforts were directed to something entirely different from their stock-in-trade. "If I did, what possible interest could that have to the Turk? He deals in entertainment, not conspiracy theories."

"These days, what's the difference? You've been spending a lot of time lately in public with an up-and-comer with the department. Given your past record, something on celluloid's in the hopper. What'd Beata promise you, a complete print of Marilyn's last, outtakes from *The Misfits,* what? If you're sitting on it for the sake of your blessed department, we'll split fifty-fifty on distribution; with a substantial fee for your mug on the Special Features; goes without saying."

"Just what are you fishing for, Teddie?"

She leaned against the door, putting in a respectable imitation of Barbara Stanwyck in anything. "I read the papers. I know as much about what happens to bombshell blondes in this business as you. Mark's burning his tires on a package deal — a bargain, if it pays out at the finish. He's paying me to get the inside track. If there's nothing to it, he's stuck with a lot of junk that goes straight to video, right along with that crap about the history of the Mafia and *Ernest Meets Gerald Ford.*"

He asked her again what she was fishing for.

"You should know. If Eleazar Sheridan didn't kill Geoffrey Root, someone else is out to kill the great blondes of Hollywood. With Marilyn, Thelma, and Jayne out of the picture, who's next? I smell an award-winning documentary, and tons of press." She struck a match off his plaster bust of D. W. Griffith and set fire to one of her eight-inch Egyptian cigarettes wrapped in brown tobacco. "I'll drop you a hint: When you throw a Hollywood party, bear in mind a hangover's not the worst thing you can expect."

"What'd you think she meant by that?" Valentino asked Broadhead, back in the latter's office.

"Don't be obtuse. You know exactly what she meant. We've been discussing it since before Padilla fixed on Sheridan."

"You mean a gathering."

Ruth, always and forever a harbinger of doom, entered without knocking. "You could save this university a ton in maintenance fees, and incidentally my heels, if you'd move all your junk into this room."

"Who's calling this time?" asked Valentino with a sigh.

"Who else? You're more popular with the Los Angeles Police Department than the Zodiac Killer."

"What line?"

"The one that's lit up, Einstein." She pulled the door shut behind her just short of a slam.

Broadhead said, "I'd ask the department to give her the sack, but she's got more tenure than I have."

Valentino punched the button. "What's up, Lieutenant?"

"A thin maybe. Computer crapped out on Morrison and Schwartz, but it pulled up a union projectionist that listed his mother as next of kin on his application; *then* it matched her to a babe that camped out in casting offices forty years ago with a portfolio of cheesecake shots. She was tanked once on a D-and-D; no other priors. Our shrink likes that kind of home environment. Got a pencil?"

"Always." He made it a point to keep a pad and a writing instrument on his person at all times. Many of his contacts were elderly, and hazy on important details regarding their careers. He always wrote down what they remembered, with an eye toward cross-referencing them with accredited sources. "Shoot."

"Not a good term to use when talking to a guy who's required to carry a firearm twenty-four-seven. Name's Arthur Augustine. He had a permanent gig at Grauman's till he refused to screen a *Blondie* marathon on the eighty-fifth anniversary of the first appearance of the comic strip."

"An exaggeration; but just slightly. As someone who would have the same argument with the head of my department, I'm loath to admit a point of agreement with a potential serial killer."

"Reason I'm calling, apart from the fact you speak the same language with these geeks, the union reports a Joe Yule, Junior, volunteered to run the projector for a party at Orson's Grill this coming Friday."

Gathering, Valentino mouthed to Broadhead. Into the receiver: "You know by now that Jerry Lewis changed his name from Joe Yule, Junior, when he went into show business. Who's hosting?"

"That's the rub. My wife talked me into seeing Kenneth Branagh's *Hamlet,* which is where I got that line. The secretary who booked the party's hiking in Alaska, in one of the nine-tenths of the state where there's no cell signal, and some dynamo of a janitor took her notes for a piece of trash. I got men combing through the refuse at Sanitation, but while that's going on I need an interpreter to interview Augustine's dear old mom. He lives with her: If I weren't convinced we're dealing with a hired hand, I'd say he fits the profile of the nutjob murderer we all know and hate."

"How soon can you pick me up?"

"This soon enough?"

Valentino got the last in stereo; through the telephone and from Ray Padilla opening the door to the office, cell in hand.

"Can I go?" Broadhead got up and hooked his tweed hat off its peg.

The house was an anomaly in twenty-first-century L.A.; white clapboard with a steep peaked roof and a picket fence, held over from the forgotten days before the movie colony was founded. Valentino half expected to be met at the door by Andy Hardy.

Instead it was opened by a woman in her fifties, with skin brown and crinkled by too many tans and a head of fried hair, aggressively peroxided. She was dressed too young, in a tight pink halter and canary-yellow Capri pants that squeezed her bare midriff into something resembling a bicycle inner tube, with a gold ring pinned to her navel. The rest was rouge, mascara, and vermilion on her fingers and toes in sandals.

"Arthur Augustine." Padilla held up his shield.

She looked from him to Valentino to Broadhead: surely the strangest trio even someone in the movie capital had seen in a spell. "Artie's at work. I'm his mother. May I take a message?"

"Where's he working?"

She drew in her chin and turned to Valentino. He pulled a sympathetic face.

"It's important we find him, ma'am. He may be of assistance in a police investigation."

"If you were any sort of police, you'd know he works at the Wilshire. He's the headwaiter there."

"Waiter?" Padilla jumped on it. "Not a projectionist?"

"Oh, that was ages ago! Running the restaurant in a hotel like that is a much greater opportunity."

The lieutenant's eyes brightened. Witnessing the event, Valentino realized the detective's mind was a cross-reference guide that rivaled the police department's mighty computer: It had been the headwaiter at the Wilshire who'd identified Eleazar Sheridan as the man who'd waited on the Limerick and Ogilvie parties; he'd had the very same connection with the victims as Geoffrey Root's partner.

Padilla unveiled yet another side of his personality. His tone became reverent. "Do you know if he was on duty the night a political fund-raiser was held for a candidate for governor some months ago?"

"If the event was important, you can be

sure he was there. They'd be lost without him. He hasn't been in an accident?" She touched her throat, a theatrical gesture.

Padilla's charm fell away. "He causes accidents."

Quickly, Valentino said, "We just want to ask him some questions. Could we see his room? He might have an appointment book. We have to be sure we don't miss his shift," he added.

"He rents an apartment upstairs. Artie's no mama's boy. You won't disturb anything? He's particular about his things."

The lieutenant let Valentino mouth the comforting response, and she stood aside. The front parlor (as it would have been called when the house was new) glittered with professional-quality photographs of a young Mother Augustine in silver frames: cheesecake shots in two-piece swimsuits, glamour poses in evening wear, tough-girl tableaus with a pistol in one hand and a cigarette dangling between red-red lips. She'd chosen to display her aspiring-actress portfolio.

"You've stumbled upon my secret," she said from the doorway. "I tested for everything in town, from soap operas to deodorant commercials. I finally landed a part opposite Bobby Darin, but I got pregnant and

230

had to bow out. Sandra Dee stepped in. I tell Artie it took my little man to knock the stars out of my eyes."

"Tease him a lot, do you?"

She tipped back her head and looked down her nose at the lieutenant. Valentino wondered if she'd had it bobbed; shiny patches on her face testified to extensive plastic surgery, recently enough to leave ruddy swellings awaiting the healing process. "He pretends to be annoyed and I pretend to think he's ungrateful, after I gave up the bright lights for him. We laugh."

"Where's his room?" Padilla said.

"Apartment." She led the way up a narrow staircase and flicked her bright nails in the direction of a closed door. Padilla tried the knob.

"He keeps it locked," she said with satisfaction. "As if I'd pry."

"As if." He produced a ring of keys from an inside pocket. "Okay if I try these?"

"Knock yourself out," she said with satisfaction.

She shot Broadhead a look. "You don't look like a policeman. Are you by chance in the industry?"

"Documentaries," he said. "We're doing a series on aging. Are you interested?"

Which visibly ended her interest in him.

The latch clicked halfway through Padilla's ring.

"Oh, my stars!" The woman's voice was a squeak.

Posters leapt out from the walls when the door was opened. Some were pricey originals, others reproductions: Marilyn Monroe sprawled before the falls in *Niagara,* Jayne Mansfield's vapid face grinning between cotton-candy hair and her ice-cream-scoop breasts in *The Girl Can't Help It,* Thelma Todd looking fetching in a lobby card for one of her comedy shorts, a chilling rendition of Sharon Tate wielding a bloody stake in *The Fearless Vampire Killers.* There were other four-color images, all of them tragic blondes: Jean Harlow, Carole Lombard, Dorothy Stratten, Inger Stevens (a suicide, in the midst of what had seemed a promising career), the long sad Parthenon of yellow hair, gaudy lives, and early death.

Someone had taken a four-inch brush and slashed a ghastly *X* in scarlet paint across every lovely face.

Oh, my stars, indeed.

24

Arthur Augustine's library, encased in steel
utility shelves decorated on the top corners
with ceramic Greek masks representing
Comedy and Tragedy; the latter painted the
same shade of scarlet as the *X* on the
doomed stars' faces), was a miniature version of Valentino's, eschewing its bright
spots in favor of the Industry's dark side:
*Hollywood Babylon, Fade to Black, Holly-
wood's Unsolved Mysteries, A Cast of Killers,
Helter Skelter.* The volumes, bound in paper,
were bloated, thumb-smeared, and dog-
eared to pages containing especially lurid
passages, all having to do with blond stars
and starlets.

A CD box atop a Sony player caught his
eye: a single of Marilyn singing "Diamonds
Are a Girl's Best Friend." It was empty.
Valentino had a good idea where its contents
could be found: in the LAPD evidence
room, with the rest of the material pertain-

ing to the Limerick homicide.

Padilla had left the group gathered in front of the grotesque shrine. He summoned Valentino and Broadhead to a small writing table, where yesterday's *L.A. Times* lay folded to a gossip column, with a check-mark beside the fourth paragraph:

. . . Holiday O'Shea, popular road-company star of *Hello, Dolly! Gypsy,* and *Gentlemen Prefer Blondes,* celebrating her 55th with husband and friends with a private screening of a local cable documentary of her life at Orson's Grill Friday . . .

Padilla looked at the archivist. "What day is today?"

The lieutenant drove with the pedal pasted to the firewall and his phone to his ear. He hit END. "That was the Wilshire manager. Augustine's on duty. The hotel's ten miles from Orson's Grill: a good half-hour in early evening traffic."

Valentino gripped the dash with both hands. "Do you think he changed his mind?"

"No, and neither did I. I told you the one thing we didn't take into account was the possibility of a hired killer. I ran it past the department shrink; he was more interested in my issues than Augustine's." Padilla banged the steering wheel with his palm. "Can't say as I blame him. Most serials do their own dirty work. This guy's got all the rage against his silly-ass mother you expect from the type, but instead of doing it himself, he has it catered. Where's the thrill in that?"

Broadhead said, "It's Hollywood, Lieutenant. Stars don't do their own stunt work. With a wannabe mom like he's got, he's probably a native. It's hardwired into him not to buck the union."

"I'm lost. Where's a hotel headwaiter figure into what we know?"

Padilla said, "It was the headwaiter at the Wilshire gave us the personal connection between Beata Limerick and Karen Ogilvie. Sheridan worked there, too, which would be where our guy got the idea to kill Geoffrey Root and finger him for it, and we fell for it like a ton of bricks. We were so sure we had the curse killer we never suspected we were interviewing him. His name's buried so far in my notes I'm not surprised I didn't remember it. Since he worked for a while as a projectionist at Grauman's, it's no big leap to figure he made contact with a colleague who moonlighted as a hit man.

"Maybe he isn't so yellow after all," he went on. "He was clever enough to cater the jobs through a second party while we worked the case according to theory. We got a squad of eggheads that studies serials and another squad that specializes in pros. They don't hang out together and compare notes."

"Nobody can know everything," Valentino said. "I get some of my best bargains from people who don't understand the value of what they have to sell."

Broadhead straightened in his seat. "So where does that leave us?"

"Let's ask the maestro." Padilla looked at Valentino. "Who was that other blonde Beata Limerick mentioned, after Marilyn and Jayne and Thelma?"

Valentino tensed. "Sharon Tate."

Padilla laid the speedometer needle all the way over to the right. The car leapt forward, brushing lesser machines from its path like dried leaves before a gale; the blasting of horns fell away in the distance.

For once, Valentino was less in fear of his life with the lieutenant at the wheel than of the consequences of driving the legal limit; in fact, he wished the machine could move faster. Whatever its speed, it couldn't match the pace of the images flashing through his brain.

Broadhead and Padilla were old enough, and their young companion enough of a film historian, to remember the lurid details of rising star Sharon Tate's murder in 1969; a ritual slaughter, along with three friends, in a bungalow in Bel Air by the Charles Manson "family" of devil-worshippers. They'd been stabbed multiple times and Sharon's blood used to smear the word "Pig" on the front door.

"At least there's one thing I can blame on you and not procedure," Padilla told Valentino. "If you'd run this past me when you first thought of it, I'd have remembered the brains behind the massacre wasn't even on the scene when it took place. Manson did it all by remote control, same as Augustine."

The man seated beside him made no response. The sun-drenched street they were racing along seemed as bleak as midnight.

25

Orson's Grill, which had rushed in, after the protean fashion of Southern California, to occupy a defunct Burger Chef on Cahuenga Boulevard, featured posters and memorabilia — the latter locked inside shatterproof glass cases — relating to the life and career of Orson Welles, with a menu engineered to replicate the late actor-director's expansive waistline in its clientele: Rib-eye steaks ringed with fat, lobsters swimming in butter, and cream sauces abounded. All about were displayed treasures such as Rosebud, the sled that had proven the key to unlock the mystery that was Charles Foster Kane in *Citizen Kane,* Welles's astrakhan official's cap from *Journey Into Fear,* a costume worn by Rita Hayworth, briefly Mrs. Welles, from *The Lady from Shanghai,* a miniature pre-production mock-up of the Viennese Ferris wheel from *The Third Man,* and the white suit Welles had worn in *Touch of Evil,* which would have fit Sydney Greenstreet in *Casablanca* and sheltered a troupe of tumbling dwarves. Many of the tables were decorated with lids from the auteur's multiplicity of boxes of consumed Cuban cigars, embalmed beneath laminate. Valentino thought that if he closed his eyes and opened his nostrils he could smell the exhaust from thousands of smokes inhaled during an equal number of hours scrounging financial backing for *Don Quixote;* a lost unfinished masterpiece the film archivist hoped one day to unveil to the public, piecemeal project that it was. Even the registration desk appeared to be a pared-down version of the prow-shaped pulpit Welles had mounted by means of a rope ladder to deliver his sermon on Jonah in *Moby Dick.*

Typical of his vocation, Valentino mused upon this late local embrace of the twenty-six-year-old New York parvenu whom Golden Age Hollywood had so deeply resented for showing them how to make movies. In the last great western boomtown, box-office profits were the sole invitation necessary to acceptance in society.

Dimly, over a concealed sound system, Welles's infamous radio broadcast of *The War of the Worlds* played on a continuous loop under *Thus Spake Zarathustra,* the theme from *2001: A Space Odyssey;* a production in which he had taken no part. Spoken dialogue unenhanced by music contributed little or nothing to the appetite. Generations earlier, the program had spread panic throughout a nation convinced that the Martians had invaded.

While the party awaited the arrival of the maitre d', Broadhead said, "If the floor show is one of Orson's magic acts, I'm outta here."

"You knew him well enough to address him by his first name?" Valentino despaired of ever plumbing the depths of his mentor's experiences in Hollywood.

"He sawed me in two once; if that doesn't qualify me, I don't know what would."

When at last the maitre d' honored them with his presence, he appeared capable of balancing out the restaurant's inspiration on a seesaw: three hundred pounds on the hoof, in a three-piece double-breasted tuxedo that might have covered the infield at Dodger Stadium when rain threatened. Unfortunately, his voice lacked Welles's celebrated timbre, as in a piping voice that apparently had never cracked, he directed them toward a private room in back.

They passed tables laden with Chicken *a la* Ambersons *Magnifique,* steak marinated in rosebuds, and bottle upon bottle of Paul Masson, of which Welles as commercial spokesman had spoken as the wine never served "before its time."

"That time being the first Tuesday after it was bottled," murmured Broadhead.

Valentino shushed him. The man was incapable of recognizing real-life drama.

A series of gasps from the seated parties they passed drew Valentino's attention to Ray Padilla, and the sidearm he'd drawn. "Is that necessary?"

"Not to worry. If I have to shoot this sonofabitch in the stomach, I'll make sure the white wine comes up with the fish."

Broadhead chuckled. "Lieutenant, I'm beginning to like you. You're living proof the Neanderthal had a sense of humor."

Padilla responded to this accolade with a verb and a pronoun.

"Classic," offered the academic.

Valentino sighed.

To a man (and woman), there wasn't a diner present whose white hair hadn't been dyed a preposterous youthful color, or whose naked scalp wasn't cloaked beneath an elaborate wig or a toupee. All told there was a million dollars of plastic surgery on display.

"Has-beens, also-rans, and wannabes." Padilla's voice was tight. "Those are Augustine's targets. Life would be simpler if these twisted jerks would just kill their mothers and be done with it."

Valentino made no reply. He was tense and his throat was hoarse from arguing in favor of the presence of two civilians at the showdown. In the end he'd compromised, agreeing to hang behind in order to avoid being trapped in the crossfire between the lieutenant and the uniformed backup he'd ordered to cover all the exits.

A burly waiter stood before the door to the back room. That was where the establishment's conceit ended. He had the build of a professional wrestler under his white dinner jacket, the pockets of which sagged beneath the weight of brass knuckles and blackjacks. Even such faded screen luminaries as frequented the place were possible targets of paparazzi and celebrity stalkers.

"Sorry, gents." His voice came squeezed through a larynx dented by fists and galvanized pipes. "Private party. Not even staff's allowed inside till after the movie."

"Whose orders?" Padilla showed him his gun and shield. The waiter blanched.

"He said he was the projectionist."

"You see a projector?"

"He was carrying a big black case like one

comes in."

"How long ago?"

A pair of muscular shoulders shrugged; they were like a rockslide settling. "Twenty minutes."

"Stand clear, Kong."

Kong stood clear.

The door was locked from the other side. The lieutenant clasped his semi-automatic in both hands and raised a foot.

"That's private property!" But the waiter/bouncer's protest was drowned out by the splintering of wood. The door was more co-operative for Padilla than Beata's had been for Valentino; he decided it was a matter of leverage and experience. It swung open, leaving a piece still connected to the frame, and banged against the wall on the other side.

"Police! Drop it!"

"They actually say that?" whispered Broadhead.

"He's a cop; they don't have to come up with clever lines." Valentino craned his neck to see inside.

Four middle-aged people in formal dress sat around a linen-covered table laden with silver and a centerpiece with reels of film elaborately interwoven among flowers, eyes wide above gags tied around their mouths.

One was a woman in her middle fifties with a chrysanthemum head of improbably butter-colored hair. She would be the guest of honor. Their hands were out of sight; tied, Valentino supposed, to their upholstered chairs.

A sallow-faced man in cords and a tweed sportcoat stood this side of the table with his back to Padilla, glaring over his shoulder at the source of the interruption. A feral expression leapt to his features. He'd stopped in the midst of drawing a collapsible steel baton — the kind modern police used in place of nightsticks — from a black leather case standing open on the table. The case was filled with long-bladed knives and coils of nylon rope.

Just then a door on the other side of the room burst open and two police officers in uniform sprang through, a man and a woman, the man standing, his female partner dropping into a crouch. Their sidearms were trained on the man holding the baton.

His head spun that way. Then his shoulders sagged and he let his weapon fall back into the case.

Padilla barked another command. The man lately known as Joe Yule, Junior, turned to face him and folded his hands on top of his head with a gesture that suggested earlier experience.

"Pigs," he said.

"What?" Padilla's tone was harsher than any Valentino had heard from him. He was a man of many parts, the lieutenant with Homicide.

The killer of three (that they knew about) shrugged.

"Your guess is as good as mine. That's the message he paid me to deliver. I take a job, I follow the client's instructions. They don't have to make sense as long as his money spends."

Holiday O'Shea whimpered through her gag.

26

Joe Yule, Junior, aka Spangler Arlington Brugh, Bernard Schwartz, and Mike Morrison, upon investigation, turned out to be one Patrick Barlow, aged thirty-six. Under that name he had a long list of felony priors, including homicide, attempted homicide, unlawful imprisonment, and assault with intent to commit great bodily harm. Although his juvenile record was sealed, the secret sources of the Los Angeles Police Department pulled up eight years in a juvenile home for suffocating his infant brother to death with a pillow at age ten. He was a known associate of a number of individuals connected with organized crime.

"Not the first in his profession to turn independent," added Ray Padilla, after furnishing Valentino with the above information over the phone. "Oh, and one of his legit jobs was with a local outfit that manufactures cosmetics for the movie studios.

That's where he learned how to make up a corpse."

"So does that close the case?"

"Don't forget his paycheck. We're staking out Arthur Augustine's mother's house and the Wilshire Hotel. If he shows, we'll nail him on suspicion, and if my faith in the LAPD pans out, we'll scrounge up enough evidence while he's in custody to send him to San Quentin, or to the maximum-security ward in the giggle house at Camarillo, which is just as likely."

"I still can't figure out why a man could resent his starstruck mother so bitterly he'd pay someone to prey on would-be starlets long past their bloom."

"Oh, I can see it. I'm not nuts, but I still got a beef with my sweet old lady for making me take accordion lessons when I was thirteen. Every couple of months I'm called down to her assisted-living community when she switches to the all-Lawrence Welk station in the community room while the rest of the residents are watching *Matlock.*"

Kyle Broadhead, overhearing the conversation on speaker while visiting Valentino in his office, said, "I bet you haul out the squeeze-box every Mother's Day and give her a concert of 'Lady of Spain.'"

" 'Amazing Grace,' actually; but, yeah. In

the old bat's defense, I have to say I'd've given Myron Floren a run for his money."

"Who's Myron Floren?" asked Valentino, when the receiver was back in its cradle.

"Worst serial killer since the Düsseldorf Ripper," said Broadhead. "There's no telling how many viewers he drove to suicide, not counting the Strauss waltzes he murdered on his accordion. I think it's on display in the Black Museum in Nashville, next to a death-mask of Fabian's voice coach."

The professor looked less shabby than usual in a rented tuxedo with a canary-yellow cummerbund and bow tie to match. The pair were clearing their desks in preparation for his wedding-rehearsal dinner.

Valentino tugged down the vest of his own evening dress; wishing he could channel Fred Astaire, who'd worn white tie and tails as casually as if they were flannel pajamas. Twice dressed formal in one month was atypical, but the sensation was no less confining. "What are the chances Padilla catches up to Augustine at home or work?"

"Slim and none. As good as our local authorities are at suppressing publicity, there were too many witnesses to Barlow's stunt at Orson's Grill. The minute CNN broke into the President's latest plea for his lost popularity to announce an arrest, our push-button killer went as scarce as a Bugs Bunny entrée at an Elmer Fudd dinner."

"That worries me. When Barlow failed to pull off a remake of the Tate-LaBianca bloodbath, Augustine's rage lost its outlet. He'll just find another Barlow, or take the next killing into his own hands."

"Who's left?"

"Who else?"

The ironclad unflappability of Kyle Broadhead gave way to a visible shudder. "Dorothy Stratten's parasite boyfriend tortured and raped her, blew off her head with a shotgun, and violated her decapitated corpse. If that's Augustine's template, he'd settle for nothing less. I can't think of a professional killer in the long black history of the trade who'd follow that plan."

"Then he'd have to do it himself." Valentino blew air. "Thank God, I can't think of anyone living who fits her profile: a *Playboy* centerfold-turned-starlet. The most recent candidate's dead of a drug overdose."

Broadhead slid his hip off the corner of Valentino's desk and touched his Tweety Bird tie. "Let's take comfort in that, and show me the way to the guillotine."

The bridegroom was in no condition to

drive (although only his closest friend could observe in his apparently unflappable exterior the subtle signs of panic), so Valentino ferried him to Harriet's apartment, where she ascended the stairs to the front door resplendent in a shimmery olive-green off-the-shoulder gown, her chestnut hair caught up in ivory combs: a gift from her beau, acquired at auction. Gene Tierney had worn them in Oriental dress in *The Shanghai Gesture,* with no more aplomb than their present owner. (The man besotted with her may have been prejudiced in this judgment, but not, he was convinced, to the point of exaggeration.)

"Do I look ridiculous?" she asked, hoisting the hem of her gown to enter the car.

Broadhead, who had moved to the backseat, said, "You're one touch short of making me reconsider my choice of bride."

"Be on your best behavior, or I'll report what you said to Fanta."

"Careful," Valentino whispered to her. "Moby Dick's about to blow."

"How can you tell?"

"Ten years working fifteen feet away from him."

They'd reserved a private dining room at the Brass Gimbal for the affair. Fanta, who might be expected to protest the choice of venue, had agreed readily, in reverence to past conspiracies launched there in the battle to save Lost Hollywood from the elements of destruction. They picked her up on the curb in front of her apartment house, a vision in a little black dress and only pearl buttons in her ears for jewelry: Valentino couldn't suppress memories of Grace Kelly. At that busy pedestrian hour, male passersby paused to look back at her, and when escorted by a female, had their biceps clenched in the grip of a dainty hand.

"You're incapable of dressing down, aren't you?" But Broadhead was visibly impressed. "I won't be responsible if some gigolo sweeps you off your feet on your way down the aisle."

"Kyle, you have the gift of insulting a girl and tying it up with a pink ribbon." She took his arm and led him toward the head table.

The room had been decorated for the occasion with framed posters advertising Hepburn and Tracy romantic comedies, *Harold and Maude, Hollywoodland,* and other motion-picture classics old and new celebrating the union of — well, old and new. Lilies and spring blossoms were intermixed in the table centerpiece, and (here Broadhead's sardonic humor had prevailed), blown-up photos of the bridegroom in mortarboard and academic gown accepting his third Ph.D., cheek-by-jowl with those of Fanta wobbling uncertainly astride a bicycle with training wheels, both knees patched with Band-Aids: The shots had been taken almost simultaneously to the day. Valentino couldn't decide if this was a product of Broadhead's sardonic humor or the future *Mrs.* Broadhead's indulgence of his bend toward the macabre.

Someone patted his arm; Harriet. "He's the kind of man who takes shots at himself before anyone else has the chance."

"Do you think he'll get over it?"

"If she can't manage that, she'll never sway a jury to her case."

It was a splendid evening. The guests, on the groom's side, included a stout revered director, with a head of astonishingly full and snow-white hair and a middle-European accent, bouncy and obviously still vibrant, but unable to find work in the Industry (with few exceptions, seventy was the cutoff date for auteurs, forty for beautiful actresses in youth-obsessed Hollywood); a stunning Japanese woman in her sixties who almost immediately upon being introduced claimed to have been Akira Kurosawa's mistress; an elaborately dignified dwarf who'd been employed as a page boy by Harry Cohn; and a pipe-smoking Brit with bad teeth and excellent bearing who'd directed second-unit for Carol Reed at Ealing Studios. All told they represented some two hundred years' experience in making movies, and their conversation, quiet though it was, convinced Valentino he'd known next to nothing about the medium he adored prior to making their acquaintance.

The bride's side was no less impressive, led by Fanta's mother, a U.S. ambassador dripping with apologies for her inability to stay long enough to attend the wedding, her services being required on the Continent before week's end. The best man had assumed she'd be a prepossessing woman, tall and aristocratic; instead, she struck him as the quintessential doting mom, short, a bit frowzy, and wearing the brocaded jacket her prospective son-in-law associated with the typical mother of the bride at every reception, sprinkled with cigarette ash. Notwithstanding, Valentino found her cheerful demeanor a refreshing break from the cynicism he often found in people who'd spent their life in politics.

"I only wish her father could be here," she said. "He actually threw himself on a grenade to save his friends in Cambodia. I've spent the last forty years trying to reconcile myself to heroism connected with a monstrous cliché."

At that moment, Valentino grasped the source of her approval of Broadhead as her daughter's suitor.

A number of unusually respectful children of both sexes, whose relationship to the parties assembled remained a mystery, rounded out the assemblage. The fare was varied, perfectly prepared, and the service several notches above excellent. The Gimbal's proprietor was an old friend of Broadhead's, a retired assistant director of some thirty years' experience, who checked in regularly in his immaculate evening dress to make sure everyone was satisfied with his meal.

Such perfection cannot maintain itself indefinitely. Just as the ambassador tapped her wineglass with a spoon and rose to deliver the first toast of the evening, Valentino's cell rang. It was Ray Padilla.

"Seen today's *L.A. Times*?" he said by way of greeting.

With a sinking heart, Valentino confessed he hadn't.

"I'll summarize: a former *Sports Illustrated* swimsuit model who calls herself Vanessa, no last name, is throwing a party in her Beverly Hills rental to celebrate the contract she just signed with Sony. They're remaking *Beau Geste* as a science-fiction flick set on Jupiter with an all-female cast. She landed the Gary Cooper role."

"I'd thought Marty Feldman put that one to rest forty years ago. He even titled it *The Last Remake of Beau Geste.*"

"Just for once spare me your bullshit education on things that don't mean doodly-squat to ninety-nine percent of the population. She's inviting her guests to stay after dinner to watch her screen test. I didn't bother to confirm if she booked a professional projectionist. I can't see Arthur Augustine passing up a chance this fat."

In an electric flash Valentino shed the magic of the evening and embraced the lieutenant's investigation. "When?"

"My bad: I swapped my morning's reading of the news of the day for an extra thirty minutes of shut-eye I haven't had since this case broke. They should be polishing off dessert right now. If I know our boy, he'll wait just ten seconds after the guests stagger on out to replay Dorothy Stratten's last date with her boyfriend. I need geek-speak to get through to a dame with stars in her eyes. Can you be there in ten? Five'd be better."

Valentino, aware of the eyes focused on

him from both sides of the table, shook loose his trusty notebook and pen. "What's the address?"

27

Valentino was predisposed to dislike the condominium where flavor-of-the-month Vanessa lived, on the evidence of superior past associations: The address had belonged to the fabulous sprawling mansion of a silent-film star whose entire *oeuvre* existed no longer, complete with an Olympic-size swimming pool, masonry carved by artisans imported from Greece, and the entire phantom cast of Griffith-era Hollywood as guests, decked out in elaborate tailoring, arriving in custom-made automobiles each a city block long. Long since gone to cranes and dynamite, the Spanish-modern-Moroccan-Italianate thumb-to-the-nose of Good Taste had been replaced with a concrete construction intended to ape the Guggenheim Museum in New York City, built in tiers separated by stripes of volcanic glass, but which in the end appeared to be a cross between a parking garage and the

Breakfast Special at the International House of Pancakes.

Valentino's compact put-put of a car was crammed to capacity with the driver, Kyle Broadhead, Fanta, and Harriet; all of whom had insisted upon abandoning the rehearsal dinner to join him in his latest adventure. No sooner had he pulled in to the curb and set the brake than they piled out like a gaggle of circus clowns dressed to attend the Court of St. James.

Ray Padilla awaited them, looking as uncomfortable as ever in his tasteful department-approved gray worsted, leaning back against his personal car.

"No backup?" Valentino asked.

"I put in for it, but the chief thinks I'm a crackpot. He might have a point. This town's rotten with naked babes wanting to be the next Julia Roberts."

Broadhead said, "I'm surprised you know the name."

"You don't know me, Doc. I'm an enigma wrapped in a puzzle with a chewy chocolate center."

He pushed himself upright, drawing his semi-automatic from its underarm holster in the identical movement. "Same setup as before, only the girls stay here."

Harriet said, "I'll tell any girls who show up."

The lieutenant pulled a face at Valentino. "Men who can't keep their women in line —"

"— were born in the twentieth century," Broadhead finished. "You know where to look for us when you need us."

"Well, hell. The closer you get up in the department, the better your chances of getting tossed to the wolves." Padilla led the way through the front door, plate glass with a chromium frame.

The elevator wouldn't go to the top floor, where they were headed, without a key. Padilla found the building superintendent in his ground-floor apartment, an Arab in a white shirt buttoned to the neck, black trousers, and glistening black wingtips, topped off with a sky-blue turban, who scrutinized the lieutenant's credentials and at last handed him a key plated in gold.

The elevator opened directly into the suite that occupied the entire top floor. As the doors slid apart, Padilla motioned to Valentino, who pressed his thumb against the button that kept them from closing. The wedding party remained inside the car as the lieutenant entered the suite.

Briefly his body blocked their view of the

scene beyond; but as he sidled away, covering the interior with both hands on his sidearm, Valentino saw a man lying on his stomach on a costly white woolen carpet, hands clasped behind his head. Standing over him facing the door, got up in one of her outlandish haute couture outfits, form-fitting, exposing one naked polished shoulder, and caught around the waist with a broad white leather belt fastened by a diamond-studded buckle, six inches taller than the frame God gave her in stiletto heels, was Theodosia Goodman, Mark David Turkus' go-to girl when it came to dealing down-and-dirty for commercially lucrative lost film classics, leveling a stainless-steel pistol the size of a toaster at the man at her feet.

"High time, Lieutenant," she said to Padilla. "When I took out that ad in the *Times,* I thought you'd have the gendarmes surrounding the block from noon on."

Padilla took a moment to find his voice; or rather the words to express his reaction.

"Where's this Vanessa?"

"You're looking at her. I placed that piece with an editor who owed me a solid. I'm the bait, and here's the rat." She kicked the man on the floor with a patent-leather toe; his whimper was an exact replica of Holiday

O'Shea's in the clutches of Arthur Augustine's hired killer.

Prostrate, the author of the most celebrated homicide case in recent memory was a narrow-gauged man in his twenties, with black hair cropped close to his skull and a pale, pimpled face gaping back over his shoulder at the lieutenant. His expression pleaded for rescue. At his elbow lay a black case like the one projectionists carried their equipment in, yawning open to expose a glittering array of cutting-edge instruments and rolls of duct tape.

"Drop the gun!"

"That's the best you can do?"

"You heard me, lady!"

"Okay, since you're so polite." Teddie Goodman seated the hammer and let the weapon drop to the carpet. "I've got a permit. Who doesn't, nowadays? I placed this man under citizen's arrest the moment I saw there was no projector in his case. The gear in it's enough to book him for carrying beaucoups of concealed weapons till you gather up the rest."

Valentino left the elevator, followed by the others. "Why take the chance, Teddie? You could've been killed."

She laughed; her laugh was too much like the rattle of a diamondback to share the joy.

"This, coming from the man whose staircase a couple of thugs threw me down mistaking me for him. I'm still wearing steel pins that set off the metal detectors every time I go through LAX. If you must know, SAG's offering a reward of ten thousand for the apprehension and conviction of the curse killer. I can invest that in Supernova and pull in ten times the amount in dividends in less than a year."

Supernova International was Mark David Turkus' corporation, a media giant that could buy and sell UCLA any day in the week. The Screen Actors Guild, financed by dues paid by billionaire stars and table-waiting hopefuls, was more than capable of making good on its reward offer. Valentino sighed; all those weeks, and all that angst, only to put his fiercest competitor another leg up on him.

The "Curse Killer" stained front pages and breaking newscasts for two weeks, complete with its familiar backstory of parental neglect and adolescent jealousy, with the added kick of a hired killer with links to organized crime; that angle alone gave the tabloids dozens of columns on the Industry's connection to Bugsy Siegel and Murder, Incorporated, with plenty of blood-stained art for illustration. It all made Valentino feel sorry for Arthur Augustine; until he thought of Beata Limerick.

Ray Padilla was forced to have his suit cleaned and pressed to wear before the cameras. When Augustine was declared mentally unfit to stand trial and remanded to the maximum-security ward of the state mental hospital in Camarillo, and Patrick Barlow was arraigned for capital murder, the entire episode began to fade, joining the shockers of Hollywood past.

Eleazar Sheridan, publicly absolved of any guilt in his companion's death, pledged his hundred thousand dollar inheritance toward the establishment of the Geoffrey Root Memorial Scholarship for talented female impersonators interested in a career in theater.

Beata's print of *The Sandpiper* went to auction. Teddie Goodman, representing Mark David Turkus, bid aggressively, but Valentino, remembering Beata now without sadness, topped her at the last minute with the unexpected backing of a representative of the U.S. State Department; a wedding present to her son-in-law, Kyle Broadhead, the head of the UCLA Film Preservation Department. The restoration experts at the university put the film on the list behind

Charlie Chan's Chance and two hundred feet of Theda Bara's *Cleopatra,* which was all of that silent feature that had come to light.

Six months after the arrests in Orson's Grill and the condo in Beverly Hills, *Dateline NBC* made Teddie Goodman a whopping offer for her story of the murderer's capture. Instead, she sold the story to Mark David Turkus, her boss, for significantly less up front, but with stock options in Supernova International. The dividends would last beyond her lifetime; not that she would leave them to anyone if she could arrange for a separate coffin large enough to contain the amount, to be buried beside her. Mark David Turkus was credited as executive producer of that project, but Teddie's name wasn't mentioned. ("She's the one person in this town who puts more store in fortune than fame," Broadhead said.) When the time came to cast the production, the directors didn't lack for has-beens, also-rans, and wannabes to fill the bill.

CLOSING CREDITS

The following sources were crucial in the writing of *Brazen,* and the Valentino series in general:

Bibliography

Anger, H. Kenneth. *Hollywood Babylon.* New York: Dell, 1981.
This is the one that started it all, releasing a flood of exposé-type books as counterpoint to the standard Dream Factory elegy, laying bare the checkered lives of movie icons. This subcategory swings between serious investigative journalism and dirty-minded trash, and for the most part thrives on the shock factor in discovering that public figures are human. Anger's text is as tasteless as the jacket photo of Gina Lollobrigida glaring at Jayne Mansfield's exposed nipple during a photo shoot, but it's a serviceable introduction to the dark side of Tinseltown. The sequel, *Hollywood Babylon*

II, presumably delivers more of the same; but I'm no more motivated to check it out than I am to sit through *Kill Bill II.*

Austin, John. *Hollywood's Unsolved Mysteries.* New York: Ace, 1970.

This one's better than the usual sensation piece hastily assembled from newspaper clippings. Long-time West Coast columnist Austin provides us with a good jumping-off point for studying the mysterious deaths of Marilyn, Jayne, Todd, et al.

Behlmer, Rudy, and Tony Thomas. *Hollywood's Hollywood: The Movies About the Movies.* Secaucus: Citadel, 1975.

Behlmer and Thomas inform us that the motion picture industry has made some two hundred motion pictures about the motion picture industry — and that tally is forty years old. The news astonishes those unaware of just how narcissistic showbiz people are. From 1908's *Making Movies: A Day in the Vitagraph Studio* through 1976's *Won Ton Ton, The Dog Who Saved Hollywood,* these chroniclers report on some of Hollywood's most notorious exercises in navel-gazing, with in-depth examinations of such gems as the satiric *Sullivan's Travels,* the endlessly entertaining *Singin' in the Rain,* and the industry-bashing *Sunset Boulevard.* (However, they fail to explain how *Boy Meets Girl,* featuring Marie Wilson — actually out-annoying the always-irritating Penny Singleton — smuggled an unwed mother past the censors.) Who better to teach us about moviemaking than moviemakers themselves? Until some confusion about rights to the use of publicity stills forced it to flee the field, Citadel was the gold standard for books on film.

Donnelly, Paul. *Fade to Black: A Book of Movie Obituaries.* London: Omnibus, 2000.

As often as I consult this book for its handy collection of facts concerning the lives of Hollywood notables, I'm reluctant to recommend it. Donnelly approaches celebrity scandal like a filthy little boy, slinging around unsubstantiated innuendo and becoming specific only when his victim is dead and unable to defend himself; in snide asides wholly unrelated to his entries, he's circumspect to the point of cowardice, but manages to snigger nonetheless, as if he's privy to something we aren't, but too coy to share. It's no surprise that he often cites Charles Higham, the master of the poison pen, from a safe distance. Higham is entirely unreliable, but Donnelly's compendium is a useful quick-search reference, so long as you separate fact from speculation.

Edmonds, Andy. *Hot Toddy: The True Story of Hollywood's Most Sensational Murder.* London: Macdonald, 1989.

Well, I'd vote for William Desmond Taylor's as the *most* sensational; but hyperbole aside, Edmonds' chronicle is the most thorough, with no book-length competition as yet, to my knowledge. A quickie TV movie was loosely based on this book, with bubblegum-blonde Loni Anderson poorly cast (not that a fortyish actress can't embody a woman who died at twenty-nine, but Anderson's sitcom training failed to give the presence required for this role). Screen it if you like — it's entertaining, as these fly-by-night affairs go — but read the book, and check out the real thing on video.

Halliwell, Leslie. *The Filmgoer's Companion.* New York: Farrar, Straus, & Giroux, 1977.

This is a reliable quick-source guide to Hollywood history, touching on individual films and providing biographical material on actors, directors, screenwriters, studios, genres, etc.

Halliwell, Leslie. *Halliwell's Film Guide.* New

York: Harper-Perennial (various).

Halliwell was a grump — a common trait of Brit pundits — particularly compared to Leonard Maltin, who seems genuinely to *enjoy* going to the movies. John Walker and others who picked up the torch following Halliwell's death in 1989 are mostly occupied in watering down his more sulfurous comments. But the details are accurate, and the entries include the names of the studios involved, an important piece of information Maltin overlooks.

Kirkpatrick, Sidney D. *A Cast of Killers.* New York: Dutton, 1986.

An anomaly, if you buy into the "blonde curse;" Mabel Norman, who suffered career suicide merely by her connection to murdered director William Desmond Taylor, was dark-haired. But this hyped-up investigation, eight decades before such bottom-feeding tell-all programs like *TMZ,* serves as the template for all the Hollywood tragedies and scandals to follow. The book, clumsily written but relentlessly absorbing, centers on aging director King Vidor's obsession with solving the sixty-year-old homicide — helped out by plucky sidekick Colleen Moore, herself a survivor of the first Golden Age of the American cinema; really, this is the stuff of a rip-roaring historical mystery. To understand the dark side of Hollywood, a country unto itself run by an oligarchy of ruthless studio moguls in command of their own private army, it's important to study this case. The money-dripping, sex-and-drug-driven 1920s Street of Dreams (which Valentino describes quite accurately as the "last western boomtown, with everything that entails") makes jaded retreads like *The Wolf of Wall Street* play like *The Wizard of Oz.*

Maltin, Leonard. *Leonard Maltin's Classic Movie Guide.* New York: Penguin, 2005.
This one's indispensable. Created to reduce poundage from Maltin's annual filmography, it provides valuable information on legendary movies made before 1960 as well as obscure titles that never appeared in the yearly guide.

Maltin, Leonard. *Leonard Maltin's 2015 Movie Guide.* New York: Penguin, 2014.
A bittersweet valedictory. Readers of Valentino know of my reverence for and dependency on this invaluable annual guide; but after forty-five years, this is the last entry. An entitled generation of gadget-users has been brought up to believe that the

fruits of a scholar's research and experience should be available to them free, and hang the unreliability of Web-based information. Leonard and I didn't always agree: He routinely assigned four stars to *The Philadelphia Story,* which I've always found stage-bound and, worse, unfunny; thought *Kill Bill* was somehow worth the price of popcorn, and found the faithful-to-the-book remake of *All the King's Men* inferior to the slapdash Cliff's Notes version that took the Oscar for Best Film in the weak year of 1949. But in the main he's been the fairest judge in a field laced with gratuitous snark.

Movies Unlimited. 3015 Darnell Road, Philadelphia, PA 19154.

Although its mention may seem like a plug, this catalogue is the most inclusive. *Every* movie available on DVD is listed in its annual eight-hundred-plus-page tome, in the same weight class with the Manhattan Telephone Directory, should such a thing still exist. The prices are competitive, and although the response time was glacial in the past, computer automation has reduced it to a fraction. Every film in every genre can be obtained through this masterful source. It has no equal, and at $9.95 plus $5.00 S&H, it's a bargain. I've ordered frequently enough to receive the catalogue *gratis;* and I'm no profligate. I'm married, after all, and must answer to a higher authority.

Peary, Danny. *Cult Movies.* New York: Dell, 1981.

A movie voyeur's treat. Although the term "cult" has been adulterated in order to lump indisputable turkeys in with genuine overlooked classics, in-depth studies of such significant misfires as *High School Confidential* are few and far between. I do, however, quibble over any attempt to include *Citizen Kane* on the same roster with *The Texas Chainsaw Massacre.* Apart from the monstrous gulf that separates them, *Kane* is far too popular to be considered a cult item. And the statement (in Peary's examination of *The Scarlet Empress*) that "it has, after all, been fairly well substantiated by most historians that . . . Catherine [the Great]'s sudden death occurred while she was attempting intercourse with a . . . steed" is ludicrous. Peary revisited his theme with *Cult Movies 2* (Dell again) in 1983 and *Cult Movies 3* (New York: Fireside) in 1988.

Riese, Randall, and Neal Hitchens. *The Unabridged Marilyn: Her Life From A to Z.*

New York: Congdon & Weed, 1987.

As good as any, and better than most, dealing as it does with established facts and eschewing pointless speculation. Conspiracy theories involving her death, like those concerning the JFK assassination, weary me. The more of them that surface, the less likely there will ever be a solution. Worse, they trivialize lives that should be judged for their best moments (averting nuclear war, say, and the pure delight of *Some Like It Hot*), reducing them to the level of a party game. The literature on this actress, by theorists as disparate as Norman Mailer and Gloria Steinem, is fast approaching that on Napoleon Bonaparte, with less justification, as it's grossly out of proportion to Monroe's brief career and her place in cultural history. I'm so jaded on this subject I've never bothered to include a book about her in my extensive library on film and film stars. Of all the sex symbols whose lives ended prematurely — with the exception of Todd — this glittering personality and fine thespian, who labored hard to perfect her craft, is the only one whose end has received more attention than her life and work. Through no fault of her own, she's become so Hollywood as to seem anti-Hollywood.

Shulman, Irving. *Harlow: An Intimate Biography.* New York: Dell, 1964.

Shulman, immortalized as the author of *The Amboy Dukes,* based this thoughtful and sympathetic account of a life remarkable for its brief brilliance in part on the reminiscences of Arthur Landau, Harlow's longtime friend and the agent who discovered her. More in-depth (and doubtlessly more accurate) biographies have appeared since, but this is one of those movie-star books that makes you want to rush out and rent anything starring its subject. Unfortunately, its success inspired both *Harlow,* a dreary and sexploitative 1965 biopic featuring Carroll Baker, and a TV movie airing simultaneously under the same title headed by an equally forgettable starlet with a similar name, Carol Lynley. It's not their fault; the ability to light up the screen is entirely natal.

Sikov, Ed. *Screwball: Hollywood's Madcap Romantic Comedies.* New York: Crown, 1989.

Beautiful women and slapstick have gone together since the days of Mack Sennett's bathing beauties, endured throughout the TV careers of Lucille Ball and Mary Tyler Moore, and remain a part of the contemporary scene thanks to Cameron Diaz, Julia Roberts, and Angelina Jolie. It may surprise those casually acquainted with cinema history just how often the sultriest bombshells fell on their prats at the behest of gifted comedic directors supported by veteran clowns. Evidence by association: Laurel & Hardy and Jean Harlow; the Marx Brothers and Thelma Todd; Spencer Tracy and Katharine Hepburn; William Powell and Carole Lombard; Clark Gable and Claudette Colbert; Cary Grant and every actress who shared his screen. Sikov's lively and informative text is the next best thing to screening *Twentieth Century* all over again; and you'll want to, along with all the others, long before you finish reading.

Skretvedt, Randy. *Laurel and Hardy.* Beverly Hills: Moonstone, 1987.

In addition to providing a precious resource of material about the immortal comedy team, Skretvedt gives us crucial insight on Thelma Todd's death, based on interviews with such surviving colleagues as Anita Gavin, and draws our attention to Jean Harlow's contribution to one of their best two-reelers, valiantly disregarding the dignity usually afforded a glamour queen.

Vidal, Gore. *Hollywood: A Novel of America*

in the 1920s. New York: Random House, 1990.

In the right hands, the historical novel is more spot-on than straight history. Vidal, who staked his claim with *Burr,* his scathing study of revolutionary America, carried that saga into the early twentieth century, with his silent-actress heroine providing a direct familial link with the narrator of that inaugural volume. He exposes the connection between the court-intrigue of the nascent motion-picture industry and behind-the-scenes manipulations in Washington, D.C. under the corrupt Harding administration, while holding out no hope that it will die with Teapot Dome. He's saying there isn't a scandal on the West Coast that hasn't its counterpart in the White House. Little has changed since the events of this story.

West, Nathanael. *The Day of the Locust.* New York: Random House, 1939.

A depressing novel, narrated by a character whom by today's standards would be committed for observation; and absolutely enthralling. West, a professional snoop who managed a residential hotel in L.A. during the Golden Age, used "research" as an excuse to open his guests' mail — to our benefit, because if it weren't for this book an important slice of Hollywood history would be lost.

Filmography

These sources are presented as a celebration of the lives (not the deaths) of some of the silver screen's most unforgettable blond bombshells. We should honor them not for their own troubles, but for the part they played in helping audiences forget theirs.

Chickens Come Home. Directed by James W. Horne, starring Stan Laurel, Oliver Hardy, Mae Busch, Thelma Todd. MGM, 1931.

Just an example; any one of Todd's appearances with these comic geniuses would illustrate her gift for humor. Along with Busch, Anita Gavin, and Lupe Vélez (another doomed actress, but a brunette, and therefore excluded from the "blond bombshell" curse; proponents of such legends are invariably dismissive of exceptions that disprove the theory), Todd was one of the few comediennes to hold their own against Laurel and Hardy. Here, she's irresistibly charming as the "winsome" Mrs. Hardy opposite Busch's nasty "blast from the past," and that same year she'd stand toe-to-toe with the Marx brothers in *Monkey Business* — a feat rare among more seasoned players. "Hot Toddy" would make her own mark in comedy shorts with Patsy Kelly, earning the pair a reputation as the "female Laurel and Hardy." Todd's untimely death may have paved the way for ditsy glamour-queen specialist Carole Lombard, but if you're superstitious or conspiracy-minded, it may also have been a blueprint for Lombard's tragic fate seven years later.

The Day of the Locust. Directed by John Schlesinger, starring Donald Sutherland, Karen Black, Burgess Meredith, William Atherton, Geraldine Page, Bo Hopkins. Paramount, 1975.

At 144 minutes, it's overlong, but a faithful adaptation of Nathanael West's book. Veteran players Meredith, Page, and Billy Barty embody the period; certain physical imperfections and stilted acting would have prevented some members of the younger cast from success in the glory days of the Dream Factory. It is, however, an absorbing story, well scripted by Waldo Salt, and the visuals helped me realize the neighborhood where Geoffrey Root and Eleazar Sheridan shared quarters.

Dinner at Eight. Directed by George Cukor, starring Marie Dressler, John Barrymore, Wallace Beery, Jean Harlow, Lionel Barrymore, Lee Tracy. MGM, 1933.

Like MGM's previous *Grand Hotel,* this is a sort of *House of Frankenstein,* corralling all of one studio's biggest box-office draws on one set. John Barrymore provides the one note of "tragic relief" in a rollicking send-up of silly society carrying on as usual in the depth of the Great Depression, with brilliant screwball turns by Harlow and Dressler, to whom falls the devastatingly funny last line. A joy to look at even with the sound off, for the outlandishly lush furnishings, lustrous Bakelite floors, and slinky gowns; but keep the volume up, or you'll miss some of the brightest and most hilarious dialogue in all of film.

The Girl Can't Help It. Directed by Frank Tashlin, starring Tom Ewell, Jayne Mansfield, Edmond O'Brien, Julie London. TCF, 1956.

Good R & B score, hackneyed plot, with professional schlep Ewell trying to make a star out of gangster O'Brien's moll Mansfield. Mansfield died tragically, but nearly as sad to say, she was no loss to the cinema. A star should be either stunningly beautiful or a good actor; in the best of all worlds, she's both, but beauty excuses the ineptitude of such as Lana Turner and Kim

Novak. Mansfield couldn't act, her legendary figure was overblown and overripe, and even after all this time her features are at best an acquired taste. She's fodder for the endurance of the belief in the "Curse of Marilyn," but in all likelihood her career would have faded from memory a generation ago but for the circumstances of her demise.

Gentlemen Prefer Blondes. Directed by Howard Hawks, starring Jane Russell, Marilyn Monroe, Charles Coburn. Fox, 1953.

The gold standard for romantic farces, with the "two little girls from Little Rock" determined to ditch show business and snag a couple of rich husbands. The music's wonderful (I happen to think Monroe was a gifted singer, but for some reason I'm in the minority; in defense of my case, I recommend comparing her voice to that of Carol Channing, who played the same role on Broadway), and Monroe's radiance, from the show-stopping "Diamonds Are a Girl's Best Friend" on, guaranteed she'd never again be billed second behind another actress.

High School Confidential. Directed by Jack Arnold, starring Russ Tamblyn, Jan Sterling,

John Drew Barrymore, Mamie Van Doren, Diane Jergens, Ray Anthony, Jackie Coogan, Charles Chaplin, Jr. (!), Michael Landon. MGM, 1958.

Van Doren indirectly inspired *Brazen;* she claimed to have given up her career to escape the Curse of Marilyn. Whether she was seriously freaked or came up with a clever face-saving spin on the cancellation of her contract, she provides an important link as a blond siren less vulnerable than Monroe and far less coarse than Mansfield, with talent to spare. *Confidential,* a claptrap of a teen-drug-exposé flick, sends Tamblyn undercover to investigate narcotics traffic in Any High School, U.S.A. Best known for Jerry Lee Lewis' pounding score ("Rockin' at the high school hop"), this one's worth watching just to see Van Doren's cat-in-heat performance as Tamblyn's nymphomaniac landlady.

Hugo. Directed by Martin Scorsese, starring Ben Kingsley, Sacha Baron Cohen, Asa Butterfield, Chloë Grace Moretz, Ray Winstone, Emily Mortimer, Jude Law, Christopher Lee. Paramount, 2011.

This is film scholar/buff Scorsese's love letter to the birth of the movies, and one of the latest in the long rich history of films about film. Based faithfully on Brian Selznick's (*there's* a name redolent of Hollywood!) illustrated children's book *The Invention of Hugo Cabret,* this script recounts an orphaned boy's attempt to connect with his recently departed father, and actual motion-picture pioneer George Méliès' journey back from disillusionment. Cohen, an intolerable nuisance in his previous outings, delivers a fine performance in a pivotal role, and Christopher Lee rounded out his distinguished career with his final appearance as a sympathetic librarian.

Liberty. Directed by Leo McCarey, Lloyd French, James Horne, starring Stan Laurel, Oliver Hardy. MGM, 1929.

In this, one of many early comedies to combine high-altitude thrills with hilarious slapstick, Harlean McGrew II, in her one scene, leaves a lasting impression in sudden undress. Re-billed later as Jean Harlow, she would underscore that effect, sometimes in the same condition.

My Man Godfrey. Directed by Gregory La Cava, starring William Powell, Carole Lombard, Gail Patrick, Eugene Pallette. Universal, 1936.

Here, Lombard paves the way for Lucille

Ball, bearing the torch for glamour-girl-as-comedienne kindled by Thelma Todd. The chemistry between urbane drifter Powell and coddled deb Lombard electrified the screen, as it did in life; Powell would continue to deliver flowers to Lombard's grave long after her death in a plane crash, notwithstanding her successful marriage to Clark Gable.

The Postman Always Rings Twice. Directed by Tay Garnett, starring Lana Turner, John Garfield, Cecil Kellaway, Hume Cronyn, Audrey Totter. MGM, 1946.

Long dismissed by *noir* aficionados as a "film *grise,*" substituting muddy gray for true black, this adaptation suffers in comparison to *Double Indemnity,* a more courageous take on another James M. Cain novel. Garfield's your cup of tea, if you like Paul Muni with angst, but Turner provides no more than set decoration as always, a lovely empty vase crowned by liquid-blond hair and no brains. She'd know her own private drama when her daughter stabbed Turner's abusive gangster lover, Johnny Stompanato, to death — although rumors persist that it was Lana herself who wielded the knife.

Red-Headed Woman. Directed by Jack

Conway, starring Jean Harlow, Chester Morris, Una Merkel, Lewis Stone, May Robson, Leila Hyams, Charles Boyer. MGM, 1932.

Although it may seem ironic to single out this title to showcase the woman for whom the phrase "platinum blonde" was coined, it's an unregenerately naughty delight, shot before the Hays Office cracked down on "questionable" content. Sleeping her way to the top without apology — and triumphing in the end — Harlow makes full use of her comedic talent, which was missing from her underwritten femme fatale turns in *Hell's Angels* and *The Public Enemy;* although our language is richer for the line she delivered in the former film: "Would you be shocked if I put on something more comfortable?" She was equally madcap and gutsy opposite Clark Gable in *Red Dust* and Wallace Beery in *China Seas* (her character drinks Beery and his seadog cronies under the table); but if Anita Loos, who also gave us Monroe's Lorelei Lee in *Gentlemen Prefer Blondes,* didn't have Harlow in mind when she created such proactive dames, it was only because the actress was unknown when she began writing. Harlow's private life was riddled with tragedy, including a husband's suicide; but her death at age twenty-six due to kidney failure was a loss from which the cinema has never fully recovered.

In his memoirs, George Hurrell, MGM's legendary publicity photographer, confessed to stealing klieg lights from an operating-room set to do justice to Harlow's unprecedented platinum coif. After her untimely death, he smuggled the lights back onto the set in respect for her memory. It was Hollywood's equivalent of retiring a baseball superstar's jersey; fittingly, in view of the blazing star's plea for privacy, he did it without fanfare.

She. Directed by Irving Pichel and Lansing C. Holden, starring Helen Gahagan, Randolph Scott, Helen Mack, Nigel Bruce, and Gustav von Seyffertitz. RKO, 1935.

Filmed at least four times, twice silent, the fourth an execrable exploitation starring Ursula Andress (a Bond girl; an express ticket to obscurity), H. Rider Haggard's fanciful tale of an immortal queen whose beauty must remain masked to avoid reducing every man who gazes upon it to helpless slavery (what woman could possibly want *that*?), is impossible to capture on film: Everyone has a different concept of just what constitutes irresistible sensuality. Gahagan (who would adopt Melvyn Douglas' surname upon her marriage to that consummate actor), came closest, although the ice-princess performance such a role would require works against fleshly desire. Gahagan's real life did not precisely end tragically, but her political aspirations dashed themselves to pieces when she opposed Richard Nixon for Congress, and took the full brunt of Washington-insider dirty tricks; to her death, she never forgave "Tricky Dick." The history of the industry is rife with *Mr. Smith Goes to Washington* naïveté come a-cropper in the face of the District in the full force of its power. It helps to explain Hollywood's spiteful jealousy regarding the political success of alumni Ronald Reagan and Arnold Schwarzenegger.

Star 80. Directed by Bob Fosse, starring Mariel Hemingway, Eric Roberts, Cliff Robertson, Carroll Baker, Roger Rees, David Clennon, Josh Mostel. Warner, 1983.

This one is Fosse (*Cabaret, All That Jazz,* the stage version of *Chicago*) at low ebb. *Playboy* centerfold-turned-starlet Dorothy Stratten's hideous sex-murder at the hands of her jealous parasite boyfriend is fodder for only the most grotesque of slasher movies; but her story's another in the seemingly endless sequence of blond bombshells come to bad ends. The horrifying details, continuing post-mortem, were too nightmarish to include in this darkest of the generally upbeat Valentino series; they make the Tate-LaBianca slayings seem almost benign by comparison. I say, let them be forgotten except in sorrow for the victim and as a cautionary tale for all those who seek celebrity at any cost.

Sullivan's Travels. Directed by Preston Sturges, starring Joel McCrea, Veronica Lake, Robert Warwick, William Demarest, Margaret Hayes. Paramount, 1941.

McCrea, a movie director in quest of inspiration, takes to the rails in the wake of the Great Depression to gather color for his magnum opus, *O Brother, Where Art Thou?* (which inspired the title of Joel and Ethan Coen's 2000 masterpiece of comedy-noir). This mixture of physical comedy and pathos (scripted also by Sturges) stands alone in the ever-expanding genre of Hollywood Looks at Hollywood. (Paramount, it should be noted, was legendary for giving maximum latitude to directors and screenwriters; in this it was unique among the studios of its time.) Lake, one of the outstanding blondes of classic cinema — her signature "peekaboo bang" hairstyle compelled Washington to ask her to change it in order to spare her imitators from catching their locks in defense-factory drill-presses during World War II — escaped the horrific tragedy that seems to have stalked the type, but died before her time of cancer in her early fifties. (The always-acerbic Leslie Halliwell, among others, scorned her "limited acting ability," but I for one find her range broader than more celebrated stars such as Lana Turner and the thoroughly inept Kim Novak.) McCrea's contribution puts the lie to *Time Magazine*'s dismissal of this gifted comedian and fundamentally decent cinema icon as a "slightly dull" leading man in his 1990 obituary. This actor's impressive *oeuvre* continues to appear in revivals decades after his death; but where, I ask you, is *Time* now?

Twentieth Century. Directed by Howard Hawks, starring John Barrymore, Carole Lombard, Walter Connolly, Roscoe Karns, Etienne Girardot, Ralph Forbes, Charles Levison, Edgar Kennedy. Columbia, 1934.

Not quite my brand of popcorn: Like Lombard and Robert Montgomery's warring married couple in Alfred Hitchcock's atypical (for him) *Mr. and Mrs. Smith,* the animosity is a little too much like life at its

288

most distressing for me to consider this one an escape. But it's a rare opportunity to appreciate Barrymore's comic timing. Off-screen, his wit was scathing, but we seldom get to appreciate it on film, which makes this a special treasure; and Lombard's energetic sparring makes her an even match. Hawks gives free rein to the comedy relief he employed to draw some of the intensity from such adventure/suspense classics as *Rio Bravo* and *Scarface* (the good version), veteran screenwriters Ben Hecht and Charles MacArthur (*The Front Page,* et al) deliver a script cut with a scalpel, and the Golden Age's deep bench of gifted character actors (Karns never fails to satisfy) round this one out just fine.

Valley of the Dolls. Directed by Mark Robson, starring Barbara Parkins, Patty Duke, Sharon Tate, Susan Hayward, Paul Burke. TCF, 1967.

This one's a whipping boy for everyone who hates big-screen soap opera, but it ages better than some more recent fare revered by critics (*The Royal Tenenbaums,* anyone?). The acting is far better than advertised — such a cast could never be mediocre, no matter how they felt about a paycheck project — and Sharon Tate stands out as a starlet dying of cancer. (Susan Hayward, as the aging diva, delivers a tour-de-force farewell to a stellar career.) The harrowing nature of Tate's murder in the Manson Family bloodbath is compounded by the fact that *The Fearless Vampire Killers* is the film she's most remembered for; Roman Polanski, its director and the doomed star's husband, was capable of helming a classic (*Chinatown*), but was more often responsible for trash like *Vampire Killers* — and for his near-Mansonesque behavior in private life. The jury's still out on whether Tate would be remembered for anything but the grotesque nature of her death. She never got the chance.

Let's raise a glass of sparkling champagne to the great blondes of Hollywood: the sacred and the profane, the damned and the deified, the fragile and the unassailable, with Harlow's line from *Red-Headed Woman:* "Blondes have more fun, do they? Yes, they do!"

The employees of Thorndike Press hope you have enjoyed this Large Print book. All our Thorndike, Wheeler, and Kennebec Large Print titles are designed for easy reading, and all our books are made to last. Other Thorndike Press Large Print books are available at your library, through selected bookstores, or directly from us.

For information about titles, please call:
  (800) 223-1244

or visit our Web site at:
  http://gale.cengage.com/thorndike

To share your comments, please write:
  Publisher
  Thorndike Press
  10 Water St., Suite 310
  Waterville, ME 04901